Silver Santa

Welcome To Kissing Springs Book 3

JOI JACKSON

First edition

Paperback ISBN: 978-1-7363163-9-9

To my Silver Santa
Thank you for supporting my crazy idea to write novels. I
appreciate you each and every day.
Love you forever,
Joi

CONTENTS

CHAPTER 1

"What is wrong with Kissing Springs?" Noemie Saint huffed to no one in particular as she grabbed her lunch bag from the packed refrigerator in the teacher's lounge at Nelson County High School. Everyone was counting down the days before the winter holiday break was scheduled to begin.

"Uh oh." Teresa Fox, glancing up from her phone, nudged her friend Dee as Noemie slammed her lunch on the table across from the two older women. "Saint's on the warpath. What happened? Did one of the kids say 'damn' in your office again?"

Dee Daniels chuckled, stabbing a fork full of spinach salad. "Heaven knows our kids don't ever use that kind of language."

Noemie side eyed each of the women. "I don't allow cursing in my safe space, but that's not my issue." She snatched open the lunch bag, pulling out an orange. "I just had a teenage boy come to my office asking for a work permit so he can apply for a job at the Kissing Springs Derby Nights Entertainment Venue."

Teresa bit her lip as Noemie stared. She didn't seem surprised.

Noemie eyed Dee next, who seemed to be intently studying the contents of her salad.

Her mouth gaped slightly. "Did you two know that Derby Nights is a strip club?"

Dropping her phone on the table with a thud, Teresa stared wild-eyed at Noemie. "Um, yeah. Where have you been? I know you just moved back to town earlier this year, but were you living in a cave?"

"Without internet, cell service or electricity?" Dee chimed in. "How do you not know about the Santas?"

"My routine is that I come here, try to steer these kids in the right direction toward being productive members of society, go see about my mother, who is not happy unless she's complaining, and then I go home for peace and quiet only to start over again the next day," she said to Dee. "I'm not out looking for men to ogle."

She had to admit though, even to her own ears, her life sounded routine and dull.

Teresa slid her reading glasses down, peering over the top of them at Noemie.

Here we go. Noemie braced herself. The older woman was not known for sugar coating her opinion.

"Saint, you need to get out and experience life! You're too young to just give up like an old spinster."

"I'm going to turn forty on Christmas Eve, I'm not that young," she pointed out.

Teresa waved her off. "Please, when I turned forty, you couldn't tell me nothing! Dee and I left our husbands at home and hit Vegas...now *that* was a male revue, even though the Santas don't do a bad job, it's a little tame compared to Vegas."

Dee nodded, tapping Noemie's arm. "Oh yeah! Teresa hit for what, two grand?" Teresa raised two fingers in confirmation and Dee went on. "I was up about five hundred, so we got dressed up like we were twenty-seven and hit the Strip! Part of that money found its way into several g-strings!" Dee cackled, giving Teresa a high five.

Teresa turned back to Noemie. "Anyway, you're divorced and about to be forty, you should be living it up. What are you doing for your birthday? We could get the other teachers and do a party bus to Derby Nights."

Dee nodded. "Yeah, I know of at least five other teachers who would go. They'd probably give us a group rate."

Eyes wide, Noemie shook her head. "Sweaty men thrusting their pelvises at me for tips, no thanks." She focused on peeling her orange. "A strip club outing for the teachers? You know, you two are kind of a bad influence."

"Saint, don't take this the wrong way," Teresa said, patting her arm again and Noemie winced. Anytime someone used that phrase, chances were good whatever came after it would be taken in the worst way. "Now, you know we love you, but I've seen nuns less uptight. You never want to go for drinks with us, you never engage in girl talk when it gets good. I'm thinking you might need a good pelvis thrusting?"

Noemie dropped the half-peeled orange, her mouth agape. "I'm not uptight." She glanced at Dee, who twisted her hand back and forth, in a "sort of" motion.

Dee cleared her throat. "Anyway, if you want to distract the boys from wanting to be strippers, let's host a career fair for the local businesses around here. That way, the kids can see there are other paths they can take."

Pointing at Dee, Teresa chimed in, "Yes, that's a great

idea! Let's do it after the holidays." She grabbed her phone and started scrolling. "I can contact some of the local businesses and see who's interested."

Noemie finished removing the rind and pulled the orange sections apart as she considered the career fair. She had to admit the idea had merit, but she couldn't let the other comments go. "I'm not uptight," she repeated firmly.

Teresa paused, not looking up. "Give me a second to send out this email." Noemie looked on in shock as Teresa's thumbs flew across the phone like she was born to text. "Now," she said, putting the phone aside, "yes, my love, you are uptight. If I had to guess, I would say you've got some pent up frustration?"

Not sure how to take the question, Noemie scowled.

Teresa sighed. "When's the last time you tended to your lady garden? Unless you've got a boy toy servicing you that we haven't heard about?"

Oh God. She wasn't having this conversation at work. She popped an orange slice into her mouth to buy some time. Although she'd never admit it, a tiny part of her was intrigued. Probably the parts they spoke of.

Between bites, she said, "My lady garden is fine, thank you. I don't need a man to be happy. I'm a professional and I conduct myself as one, that's all."

"True, you don't need a man to be happy," Dee added, snagging an orange slice from Noemie's napkin, "but you do need a good vibrator. Make that investment and you'll see. You'll be walking through the halls singing like Julie Andrews in "The Sound of Music"."

"Listen to Dee, Saint. She's right. That'll unwedge that huge stick up your ass. The party store has a good selection, you should go check it out," She glanced back down at her phone. "Oh, I've gotten a couple of responses about the career fair already. I'll set up a planning meeting before we break for the holidays."

"Wait, the party store sells adult toys?" Noemie couldn't wrap her head around that at all. "This place has certainly changed since I left." Having recently relocated back to town, she'd stared in awe at the progress in Kissing Springs. "So many tourists now. And the traffic gets bad. Almost like I was back in Charlotte."

Teresa stood. "Yep, thank Derby Nights for that." She glanced at her watch. "I've got lunch room duty, so I will see you girls later. Saint, let me know when you're free for the career fair planning meeting." With that, Teresa sauntered out of the lounge.

Dee turned back to Noemie. "We'll go check out the toys with you one lunch hour if you want. Teresa knows all the good brands."

Noemie rose, tossing her orange peels in the trash. "Ah, thanks for the offer, but I'm fine."

After lunch, Noemie hurried into her office, a small room that was always too cold in the winter and too warm in the summer. She hid a contraband space heater in her lower desk drawer and only brought it out when the Kentucky weather made the room unbearable.

There were only a few days until the winter holiday break started, and it was so cold the office could safely store the school's meat supply. Noemie absently rubbed her hands together for warmth after starting the heater, thinking about the other teacher's words.

She was *not* uptight. *Was she?*

While Noemie normally didn't engage in the raunchier teacher's lounge conversations, she also didn't shy away from saying those topics shouldn't be discussed in the workplace, especially where they were surrounded by young, impressionable ears.

All the teachers knew she didn't allow cursing around her and she maintained, or at least tried to anyway, a sense of professionalism in their school. She knew the jaded older teachers rolled their eyes at the notion, but Teresa and Dee had become her champions with them. The newer teachers, who didn't know any better, fell in line quickly.

Granted, there were a couple of girls she knew of who could teach a course on The Joy of Sex, based on some text messages she'd intercepted, but they were the exception, not the rule. Still, the conversations were too much for the workplace.

She was pretty sure the conversations resumed once she was out of earshot and part of her, she admitted, felt left out. Not that Noemie could offer anything relevant. As she'd grown up in a strict Jehovah's Witness household, then married a conservative, devout God-fearing man, her knowledge about sex was basic at best.

Alone in her office, she could freely confess to herself that she'd never gotten the big deal about it. Noemie had never experienced the hot, sweaty, lusty sex prevalent on movies and television shows. She'd never, to her knowledge, had an orgasm. She wasn't sure she could. And she'd made her peace with that.

Or so she thought.

CHAPTER 2

"*I* signed you up to speak to the students at Nelson for Career Day."

Jameson Mitchell dragged his attention from the payroll report he was reading to glare at his mother, who walked into his office and plopped down in the seat across from his cluttered desk.

Her eyes, the color of warm brandy, narrowed in challenge, daring him to protest.

He knew that look well. Sighing, Jameson closed the laptop. In his youth, he'd been brazen enough to challenge his mother, but now that he was in his mid-forties, he knew better. The woman stood at an inch over five feet on her best day but commanded attention when she needed to, which was 99% of the time.

"What Career Day? When? And how do you know I'm available?" He motioned at the fitness center. "I do have a business to run."

She waved a dismissive hand. "Teresa Fox just sent me an email saying they want to organize a career day for the

7

students and they need the small business owners of Kissing Springs to participate. I said to myself this is a perfect opportunity for J&J Fitness to get an intern or two to help out, especially during wedding season when the Santas are in here rehearsing. Plus, I could use an assistant."

Jameson leaned back, crossing his arms over his chest. *This should be interesting.* "Ma, you're only here part time. What could you possibly need help with?"

She sniffed. "Keeping this place clean! You know there are a few bad apples that don't wipe the machines off once they use them. That's why I use my gloves when I lift."

His mother had recently started taking strength training classes with her friends. The few times Jameson had made the rounds during their sessions, there was more gossiping going on than lifting, but he wasn't about to point that out.

"Ok, an intern might make sense, but I don't know that you need your own personal assistant. And when is the career thing? Don't they get out of school soon?"

Jameson watched as his mother dug her phone from her back pocket and squinted at the screen. Her reading glasses, as always, were propped on the top of her head. "Teresa says if they get enough interest, they're holding a planning meeting before school lets out for the holidays. I told her either you or I would be there to represent the best gym in Kissing Springs," she said proudly, "but you'll probably need to go. I've got too much on my plate these days."

"This is the only fitness center in Kissing Springs," he reminded her. "I asked Dad about coming by to have a beer with me one evening, and he said he would have to let me know later. What keeps two retired people so busy?"

"I'm trying to get the house ready for the holidays and the toy drive is coming up. Then Jordyn will be done with her finals and home before you know it." She touched her head.

"Oh, that's where I left my glasses. Anyway, that sister of yours said she might grace us with her presence this year and then your father and I are going on our cruise right before New Year's."

She heaved a heavy sigh and Jameson raised an eyebrow at her dramatics. "It would be nice if you could get a student in before I leave, but I don't think we have enough time. Now then, when you go to the meeting, you ought to stop by and say hey to Noemie. You know she's the new guidance counselor."

Jameson's stomach dropped, but he kept his face neutral. He was sure the last thing Noemie wanted to do was rehash old times with him. "How's she doing? I know her father's death probably hit her hard."

Part of him wanted to see Noemie. Wanted to apologize for everything and see how she was adjusting to life back in Kissing Springs.

But the other part didn't have the courage to face her yet.

"Haven't seen her. You should go find out for yourself." His mother paused, toying with the buttons on her cardigan. "I believe she's still single...maybe you could ask her for coffee?"

Jameson ran a hand over his chin. "Ma..."

"I know, stay out of your love life, but Jordyn is grown and in college. You don't have to worry about taking care of her so much. You can finally get a life of your own. I always thought y'all were perfect for each other."

"Ma, that was twenty years ago. We're different people now." Back then, he'd fallen hard for Noemie, crafted dreams of their life together once they graduated from college, but thanks to him, those dreams evaporated.

His mother pursed her lips. "I realize that. I said ask her

for coffee, I didn't say you should propose. Go see what you can see."

What did that even mean, 'go see what you can see'? He shook his head.

As if reading his mind, she continued. "Go ask how she's doing, if she's dating anybody, that sort of thing. See if you still like her. I remember you were crazy about her that summer when you were in school.

"Anyway, I'm not trying to run your life." She rose. "I'll send your contact info to Teresa. Let me know when the planning meeting is scheduled. I'm gonna wipe these machines down and get the studio ready for the yoga class. Think about my personal assistant, son."

Running his life was exactly what she was trying to do. Jameson watched his mother as she strode around the floor, speaking to the members working out.

He gave up on trying to get any real work done for the moment as his thoughts shifted to his ex-girlfriend, Noemie.

Small towns being what they were, he knew via the locals exactly when she'd moved back to town and while she didn't live with her mother, she visited often. She had opted to rent an apartment from one of the women who frequented the gym, so he'd pretty much known that as soon as the lease was signed.

Not that he'd been actively keeping tabs on her. People in town knew they had history and they kept him up to date without him having to ask. Who needed social media when you lived in a small community?

He also knew she was divorced.

Jameson got up from his desk and stood in the doorway, greeting members as they trickled in for the yoga class.

He wondered if she was as knowledgeable about him. Did she even care? Probably not, especially after all these years.

Noemie wasn't one to share a lot of details about her life as he remembered. The locals hadn't seen her out and about at all, so this career fair was a perfect way for him to at least say hello and see how she was fairing being back in town. An abandoned hand weight on the floor caught his attention and Jameson rushed over to put it back where it belonged. He needed to stop romanticizing the past. He had been the one to break things off with Noemie after a summer fling. Which was for the best. They were essentially from two different worlds, even back then. She was home from college at Spelman in Atlanta and he was working his way through junior college, trying to figure out what he wanted to do with the rest of his life and struggling to pass a basic College Algebra class.

Jameson returned to his office. He should be reviewing the trainer schedules for the upcoming week or making sense of the mess on his desk. He glanced at the picture of his daughter on his desk. The picture, one of Jordyn in her cap and gown, was now almost a year old.

Jordyn was wrapping up her first semester of college in a few days. She'd told him she was finishing up her finals and would be heading home as soon as she turned in the last assignment. He couldn't wait to see her. While he'd encouraged Jordyn to attend any school she wanted, he secretly hoped she'd stay close and go to the community college in town like he had, so she could continue to live at home. Now she was miles away in Lexington at the University of Kentucky, and he had to rely on text messages and video calls to stay connected.

His baby girl was growing up and would soon have a life of her own, he realized as he stared at the picture. Jameson shook the thought out of his head. Yes, that time was coming, but for now, he could focus on welcoming her back. They needed to get a tree and decorate the house, activities she'd made him promise he wouldn't do without her.

Shifting his thoughts from his daughter, he considered his mother's words. Maybe she was right and he should ask Noemie out for coffee.

CHAPTER 3

$\mathcal{T}$he day of the planning meeting for the career fair started off hectic for Noemie and went downhill from there. On the drive to work, she'd spilled coffee on her favorite cashmere sweater and had to go back home to change, then she'd gotten to school late only to find that half the school was searching for her.

A student rumored to be pregnant had fainted in class and needed a place to recover, as well as the services of the school's only counselor.

Noemie retrieved the student from the nurse's office, which was chaos after a fight broke out that several students jumped into, and sat the girl down with a carton of milk from the cafeteria.

They talked for a while and Noemie was able to pry the truth about the girl's condition from her. She'd started the rumors herself because she was hoping to get removed from her home.

Noemie's heart broke for the student as she listened to

the girl talk about her family. She scheduled time to talk to the girl's mother and eventually sent the girl back to class.

Once her office was empty, she had just enough time to snag another cup of coffee before her next meeting.

She was on her way to her meeting, hot coffee in hand, when Teresa waylaid her in the hall. "Saint, we've got a situation. Dee is heading home for the day; she's thrown up everything but the kitchen sink, and my daughter just called in a panic to ask if I could pick up my grandson from daycare this afternoon," she exhaled. "Which means we either need to reschedule the career fair planning meeting today or you run it on your own."

"I can run it. I've got a couple of student assistants who can help me. Tell Dee I hope she feels better," Noemie said, mentally adjusting her to do list. "We can all sync up tomorrow or whenever Dee's back."

Teresa looked relieved. "Thanks. I was hoping you would still hold the meeting. I brought cookies and bottled water. They're in the fridge and you should have the agenda already. I'll send you the list of people who said they would come. Let me know how it goes."

Nodding, Noemie hurried to her next meeting.

An hour before the career fair planning meeting, Noemie, feeling like she had been playing catch up all day, strode into the STEM Innovation Center, the school's newest addition, to get everything set up.

She'd asked a couple of her student assistants to help and tasked them with making the table look more festive using leftover red and green napkins from last week's faculty potluck and a red tablecloth snagged from the local dollar store.

The two students had created a cute display for the cookies, bottled water and coffee, she nodded in satisfaction.

Checking her watch, Noemie saw that they had a few minutes before the guests were scheduled to arrive. Teresa sent the list of attendees before she left for the day and Noemie had printed the list so that participants could sign in.

She'd barely had time to review the list, but she scanned it, curious to see who might be attending. J&J Fitness stood out from all the other businesses on the list.

Noemie would never admit it, but she'd looked up her ex, Jameson, shortly after moving back to town. Telling herself it was curiosity and nothing more, she saw online that he'd opened a gym and she'd read about the grand opening and how he'd named it after his daughter and himself.

There was a picture of him on gym's website and she'd spent more time than she should have studying his picture, wondering if the image was recently taken.

He looked good. If she didn't know better, she'd assume he was hired to model for the website and marketing material.

She'd breathed a quick sigh of relief that Jameson's mother, Carla Mitchell, and not Jameson, was attending.

She was *not* ready to see Jameson.

Since J&J Fitness would be participating in the event, she'd have to see him eventually, but that was after the holidays. She'd deal with that stress later.

Hustling over to the faculty ladies room, she smoothed her hair and checked her makeup in the mirror. Noemie gazed at her reflection. She wasn't as small as she was back in college. Her hair wasn't as thick and she had noticed a few

JOI JACKSON

grays. *It's all a part of getting older and wiser,* she assured herself as she walked back toward the Tech Center.

The student assistant tasked with manning the entrance to make sure everyone invited to the meeting knew where to go flagged her down as she neared.

"Hey Ms. Saint! There's only one person here so far and he's asking for you."

Hiding a smile, Noemie appreciated the girl's eagerness. "Thank you, Olivia. I'll go say hi."

Once she entered the room, a man strode over to her, sticking his hand out. "Ms. Saint?"

She nodded and he continued. "I'm Dr. Trevor Hendricks. I opened up a dental practice on Main Street a few months ago. You've probably heard about me? We donated to the toy drive."

Noemie raised an eyebrow, shaking his proffered hand. Yep, the parents and teachers organizing the annual toy drive for Kissing Springs families in need had a lot to say about the odd donation from the town's newest dentist. "Of course. Thank you for the generous donation, Dr. Hendricks."

While she knew every donation helped, she couldn't help feeling bad for the children hoping for toys to open on Christmas morning who would instead be getting enough dental floss and toothbrushes to last them for the next few years. She'd add a few more toys herself and see if she could squeeze more donations out of their bigger corporate sponsors.

He beamed at her, still holding her hand. "You're very welcome. And call me Trev."

Noemie started to say something but found the man was staring intently at her mouth. "You've got very nice teeth, and I've got this new whitening product that would make them perfect."

16

She pulled her hand away, covering her mouth self-consciously. "Um, thanks, I haven't had a chance to make any dental appointments yet since I've moved back to town, but maybe after the holidays?"

"Of course, let me just show you some before and after pictures," Trev pulled out his phone, quickly scrolling through the photo gallery.

Looking around desperately trying to find a reason to pry herself from the teeth whitening sales pitch, Noemie wished Teresa and Dee hadn't left her to handle this event alone.

"So, right here, this woman is a heavy coffee drinker, which is one of the major causes of tooth discoloration." Trevor held his phone out for Noemie. "It's like we took ten years off her age just in whitening her teeth."

Noemie glanced down at the before and after picture. "Very nice. Do you have a business card? I need to check on the students at the front door." She gave him an apologetic look.

Trevor whipped a card and pen from the pocket of his blazer. He then turned the business card over to the blank side, scribbling quickly. "I'm putting my personal cell number on here, in case you want to reach out after hours. I hear you're single," he pressed the card into her hand, "maybe we can go out for drinks one night?"

Glancing up in irritation, Noemie started to tell the man she wasn't interested in the teeth whitening or drinking with him when she heard a voice behind her that sent shock waves radiating from her toes all the way up to her heart. Before she could recover, she felt a large hand on the small of her back.

"Hey Noemie, sorry I'm late."

The first time he said her name, back when they were

younger, he'd dragged it out, making sure he pronounced it correctly. "No-em-mee?" he said, his eyes fixated on hers.

Her name rolled off his tongue like a soft caress and had her wondering what it would sound like if he'd whispered it in her ear. She had nodded, unable to form words and unsure what the warmth flowing through her meant when he said it again, the proper way this time, and asked her what it meant.

She cleared her throat. "Oh, um, it's French. It means pleasant," she said more breathlessly than she liked.

He nodded, not taking his eyes off her. She'd looked away first, feeling like she was being tugged under rushing water.

Here they were, twenty years later, and Jameson's presence had the same effect on her senses. Warmth from his hand on her sent a wave of familiar awareness through her and she stepped away slightly, annoyed at her primal response.

Jameson moved around her, thrusting his hand toward the dentist. "Jameson Mitchell, I own J&J Fitness."

Trevor introduced himself as the men shook hands. Noemie could tell Jameson didn't care for the dentist, even though he greeted him pleasantly enough. Jameson's jaw was clenched, and he was grasping the other man's hand like he wanted to slam him to the ground.

She allowed herself a moment to regard the older, grown-up Jameson. Not surprising, he still towered over her and although he had a lot less hair now, the bald-with-a-beard look suited his deep brown complexion. He was wearing a well-cut sport jacket and khakis, exuding the confidence of a successful entrepreneur. The picture on his website hadn't done him justice. He looked even better in real life.

She tilted her head, intrigued by how well she could still read his face.

He was scowling at Trevor and trying to hide it, his full lips pressed into a firm line.

Those lips. Without thinking, she raised a hand to her own lips, recalling precisely how good his felt on hers. She wondered if they had changed much over time.

Noemie shook her head to clear the images of them stealing kisses between classes.

Enough of that. She wasn't going to stand there gawking. "Gentlemen, please help yourselves to the refreshments. I need to go check on the students. We'll get the meeting started in a few minutes." With what she hoped was her best hostess smile, she left them and strode to the entrance.

Once everyone was in the room, Noemie stood at the front of the classroom style setup, waiting for the participants to take their seats. Jameson chose a seat at a desk in the front of the room, directly in front of her, and she sighed inwardly. Of course, he decided to sit there, of all places. She'd need to stay focused.

He slipped out of his jacket to reveal muscular arms and a massive chest under a J&J Fitness golf shirt. She wasn't into body builder types, so she shouldn't have been impressed. She shouldn't have the urge to run her hand over that chest, should she?

She blinked, forcing her attention back to the notes in her hand. *Focus, remember?*

Right.

Clearing her throat, Noemie waited for the group conversations to quiet.

Jameson's gaze never left her face. She turned away from him, directing her attention on two women sitting to her left and introduced herself, then asked everyone in the room to introduce themselves and their business. "Thank you all for coming out. I'm pleased to see so many businesses from the community interested in participating."

She had the group's full attention. "I grew up here in Kissing Springs. I attended this school, so I'm proud to be back as the guidance counselor to help our students pursue their dreams. While I have nothing against the town's efforts to increase tourism, I have recently had too many young men aspiring to work at Derby Nights for comfort. If the girls wanted to become strippers, there would be a lot more outrage and intervention and, frankly, I don't understand why we are encouraging our teen boys to take off their clothes for pay."

A woman in the back raised her hand. "Don't the dancers have to be at least eighteen?"

Noemie nodded. "Yes, they do. The problem is that the high school boys who aren't of age are asking me about work permits and trying to get fake IDs so they can work there. We need an alternative, and that's where you all come in."

Trevor spoke out. "There's a male strip club in this town?"

Noemie saw Jameson rub his head in irritation.

Jameson folded his arms. "Most people do their due diligence before opening up a new business in a new town. It's not like Derby Nights is a speakeasy."

Trevor glared at Jameson's head but kept silent, which Noemie thought was a wise choice. The man had a good six inches on the dentist.

"A lot of us benefit from all the bachelorette parties hosted here," another woman interjected, "which is the reason we can offer these kids jobs."

Trevor cleared his throat loudly. "I'm with Ms. Saint. We need to show the kids that there are plenty of opportunities for them outside the strip club."

Jameson rolled his eyes. Noemie sighed. These two grown men reminded her of her students.

Her lips pursed, Noemie forced herself to stay calm and get the meeting back on track. "I think they're setting their sights too low. Anyone can take their clothes off for money, but the boys who have approached me have so much more potential. I don't want them getting caught up in that lifestyle."

"You know the Santas aren't sex workers, right? They're trained dancers," Jameson countered.

Noemie crossed her arms. "I'm sure they are professionals, but I think they send a bad message to the kids."

Jameson directed his words at Noemie and the dentist. "Beth has a point. Derby Nights has put this town on the map and because of their success, most of us have been able to start and run our businesses. The guys train at my gym. The women coming in for the parties get their nails done at Ruth's place. They eat at Aunt Minnie's Pie Shop. They are supporting all of us and we're thankful."

A woman in the back stood up. "You might have grown up here, but you've been away too long. The town has changed. Maybe you should do your research before you come in turning your city nose up at the country bumpkins."

There were a few nods and half-hearted claps of agreement.

Noemie stared, shocked. *Is that how the town saw her?*

Jameson stood, turning toward the back. "Ok, now, we don't need to make this personal. Let's keep things professional." He turned back to Noemie. "Since I assume you didn't call us all here to debate on the morality of Derby Nights, what do you need us to do? When is the career fair?"

Composing herself, Noemie glanced at the notes she'd prepared. "We'd like to hold the career fair right after the holidays. If some of you need students to intern, that would be great." She looked around at the crowd and sent Jameson a look of gratitude. "I certainly didn't mean to offend anyone. I love this town and missed it while I was away."

The group came to a consensus on the date, time, and agenda for the fair, then the meeting adjourned. Most of the participants shook her hand and thanked her for organizing the event.

When the woman from the back approached, she narrowed her eyes at Noemie. "Before you judge the Santas, you should check out one of the shows. It might loosen you up some." With that, the woman slung her handbag over her shoulder and prepared to exit the room.

Noemie recoiled, as if the woman had slapped her.

Jameson stepped up to the desk where Noemie stood. "Brenda, come on, we're all working toward the same goals here. Now, when are you going to come by for the next mindful meditation class?" he asked the woman. "The class isn't the same without you."

The scowl she wore melted as she turned to Jameson. "Really, I just haven't had time lately. I'm helping Cam with the kids, but I'll try to stop by next week."

"Good, I'll look for you. Brenda, have you met Noemie?" Noemie watched Jameson place a hand on the woman's arm. The woman's fluttering eyelashes in response to the touch nearly made Noemie snort, but she managed a gracious smile and held out her hand.

Brenda stared at Noemie's hand for a beat before placing her own in it. "No, we haven't met," she said reluctantly. "Brenda Leeds. My son is one of the Santas and I do some costume work for them."

Noemie let out a nervous breath. "I'm sorry, Ms. Leeds, I really meant no disrespect to the Santas."

Brenda pursed her lips. "None taken. I do think you should check out the show, I know I'm biased since my son is in it, but it's still good entertainment." She turned to Jameson, who was doing a bad job of hiding his grin. "I'll try to get by next week. You hold my spot, Jameson." She gave him a flirty wave as she walked toward the exit.

Always the charmer. She envied that quality in the man standing in front of her. She hadn't asked for his help, but she appreciated him smoothing the feathers she'd ruffled. "Thank you."

He shrugged like it was no big deal. "That kind of energy wasn't going to get us anywhere." He peered at her, making her feel like she was being assessed like a lab experiment and found wanting. "How are you? Looks like the last twenty years have treated you well."

She glanced down self-consciously. "I've not missed any meals, as you can see. But I suppose I can't complain. How about you? You look like the years have been great to you."

That was an understatement. The man aged better than a fine wine. When she first met him, Jameson used cockiness to mask his insecurities, but now she could tell he was confident in who he was: a successful business owner who still turned heads when he entered a room. Noemie hadn't missed the appreciative looks he earned from the women at the meeting.

Be careful around that one, her logical brain warned. *No need for him to break your heart again.*

CHAPTER 4

*H*er comments threw him. She was clearly insecure about her weight, even though he thought she'd filled out nicely since he'd last seen her. Back then Noemie was very thin, almost too thin for his taste, but now, he glanced casually at her again, she was curvy and thick in all the places he liked.

He frowned. He shouldn't be leering at her like a dirty old man.

As the participants made their way over to her and as she thanked them for coming, Jameson focused on her face. Her dark brown, expressive eyes had been one of the first things he'd noticed about Noemie when they first met. He used to be able to read her emotions by looking into her eyes, but they were hooded now. She was pursing her lips, making him recall how badly he'd wanted to kiss them back then.

The dentist ambled up, grinning stupidly at Noemie as he shook her hand. Jameson watched their exchange. Noemie crossed her arms, stepping back when he pushed into her personal space, her body language radiating that she wasn't interested, but the man couldn't, or wouldn't, take a hint.

His patience thin, Jameson spoke. "Sorry to interrupt, Ms. Saint, I'd love a tour of the new innovation center before I leave, if that's ok? I've heard it's one of the best in the state."

Trevor glared again. "Well, I've got an important dinner with clients tonight, so I need to leave, but Ms. Saint, don't hesitate to call me if you need anything. It's imperative we get the young men of this town on the right path."

Once everyone was gone, Noemie turned back to him, her eyebrow raised. "I was waiting for one of you to lift a leg and mark your territory."

"We cavemen can be civilized when we want to. At least I can." He met her eyes. "You're looking well. I guess marriage agrees with you?"

She threw him a look. "I'm sure you heard through the little biddie committee the minute I filed for divorce. There are no secrets in this town." She jerked a thumb toward the exit. "Even the new dentist knows I'm single."

Noemie was right. His mother was a card-carrying member of the town busybodies, retired women who volunteered on all the committees and boards they could find.

He shrugged. "Just making sure. You could have remarried."

"No, once was enough." Noemie crossed her arms, clearly indicating she was no longer speaking on that subject. "How's your mother doing, by the way?"

"She's good. She helps me out in the gym a couple days a week by terrorizing the members."

He leaned in, lowering his voice. "How's your mom holding up? I wanted to come to your father's memorial service, but I didn't know...I didn't want to disturb you. I'm sorry for your loss."

She looked away, uncrossing her arms. "Thank you. We got the flower arrangement you sent. That was very thoughtful of you."

They stood silently. Jameson wanted to, well, he didn't know what he wanted to say or do right then. Part of him felt he should let sleeping dogs lie and keep the past in the past. But another part wanted to apologize for the pain he'd caused her back then.

"How have you been? You getting settled in?" He asked and immediately regretted the question. Hadn't they already established that she was good?

"I'm trying to. The town has changed so much on one hand, but there are some things that will probably never change. This high school, for example, seems so much smaller than when I went here. But they've got this STEM Innovation center now and the kids are so much savvier than we were. Still, they are high school kids with teen problems." She shrugged. "I'm rambling. To answer your question, yes, I'm settling in ok."

Noemie thrust her hands in her pockets and walked toward the window. "I didn't know people were so passionate about the Santa strippers. I guess I stuck my foot in my mouth today."

"I mean, yeah, Derby Nights is a big deal. They bring in more tourism and people are working again, starting small businesses, it's revived the town, so people have strong opinions. Probably not what you're used to coming from Charlotte, but for us, it is."

She turned to him, dropping her hands to her sides. "Am I coming off like I'm some uppity stuck-up witch now? I didn't mean to insult anyone; I just don't get why anyone would want to strip for a living. It's vulgar and wrong."

Jameson smirked at her word usage, recollecting that she didn't curse and would quickly call out anyone who did.

"Noemie, you're entitled to your opinion, but you can't judge these people. Not if you want to help the kids." He felt the frustration rising in him. Noemie had always been headstrong; he recalled what she'd said earlier about things changing and yet staying the same.

"I think as much as I tell myself I don't want to turn into my mother as I get older, I'm headed down that path." She walked back toward him. "Jameson, it was nice seeing you again." She stuck out a hand to shake his.

He glanced at her hand. "Come on now, we've known each other too long. Let me get a hug."

Jameson opened his arms. Noemie hesitated a beat, then wrapped her arms around him. Jameson held her, sneaking a peek at her bottom half. He could see the curve of her ass underneath her oversized sweater. Yep, he confirmed, the extra pounds she was fretting about were right where they needed to be.

Noemie felt good in his arms. He inhaled, enjoying the soft rose scent she wore. He decided he should back away before he did something stupid like kiss her senseless. He didn't want to get slapped.

He clasped her hands as they stepped apart, taking her in. "Ms. Noemie Saint is all grown up."

With a smile on her face, she rolled her eyes. "Yep, grown and being an adult, that's me."

She dropped her hands from his, inching toward the door. "I'm going to see about my mom before it gets too late. She complains about me driving around after dark."

"I can follow you over in my car if that will help," he said, even though he knew she wouldn't take him up on the offer. She'd always had an independent streak.

Waving him off, Noemie said, "No, no, that's fine. I'm sure you have better things to do." She approached the desk where the cookies were. "Do you want any of these? If not, I'll put them out in the teacher's lounge tomorrow."

Jameson patted his stomach. "Nah, the teachers can have them. I've had more than my share already."

They stood together. Jameson wanted to know more about her life since he'd last seen her but he didn't want push. She seemed like she wanted to ask him something but neither of them spoke. Like a game of silent chicken. Jameson saw Noemie surrender first. "Thanks again for agreeing to speak at the career fair. I'm going to go check on my mom."

She gathered the remaining cookies, her tote bag, and stood at the door, waiting on him. He realized she wanted him to leave so she could lock up. Jameson nodded and left the room. He watched her lock the door.

Once they were in the hallway, he offered to walk her to her car. Her car, he assumed, was parked in the faculty lot while he was closer to the front of the school in the visitor's spaces. It would be a trek for him, but he didn't mind. The late afternoon was warm for December and a brisk walk would do him good.

"You don't have to do that. I'm fine. This is Kissing Springs, not New York City," she said, tugging her tote closer to her.

Jameson shrugged. "I really don't have anything better to do. My daughter isn't due home for the holidays until her finals are over, so I'm going home to an empty house."

Noemie nodded. "I'll be fine, really. You've done enough today. You should go home and relax, or whatever you do in the evenings."

"I'll just follow you in my car and make sure you reach

your mother's house ok," he said, leaving no room for argument.

Noemie started to say something, then stopped.

Jameson knew she was going to argue before she opened her mouth. He pushed on. "Look, I'm just trying to be a gentleman. Humor me."

She sucked her teeth. "I have been back in Kissing Springs for a few months now and in that time," Noemie heaved her tote back onto her shoulder, "I have managed to get myself to and from work and my mother's house and my father's gravesite just fine. I have a phone with GPS on it and I can read street signs. Right now," she whipped her phone out of a pocket on the front of the tote. "My mother's house is literally a ten minute drive, which I would have already done by now if I wasn't standing here trying to convince a man I haven't seen in twenty years that I'm an adult now. I am good. Have a wonderful evening." With that, she turned and strode toward the door.

Jameson grunted. He got the whole independent woman thing, hell, he was trying to raise his daughter to depend on herself, but this "I don't need a man" thing was getting out of hand. "Fine. You have a good evening as well, Ms. Saint."

She turned back around to face him. "I need to escort you out of the building."

He held his hand up in an "after you" gesture and followed her out the door.

On his drive home, he sulked. *Damn women.* This was why he didn't do relationships. He was just trying to do the right thing and make sure she got to her mother's house safely and she snapped like a turtle for no reason. He didn't recall her being so feisty that summer when they met. Back then, Noemie Crawford was sweet, smart, and fun to be around.

The Noemie he encountered now was short tempered, judgmental, and spoke her mind.

She was also stunning. Long, black hair, expressive dark brown eyes that reminded him of an aged cognac, smooth cocoa brown skin, and a smile that would melt an icecap. Yep, Noemie was all grown up now.

He found himself gearing up for a challenge. *Challenge for what?* he wondered suddenly. He wasn't chasing anybody or accepting any thrown gauntlets. His mission was to get his daughter through the next three and a half years of college and keep his gym profitable.

That was it.

Noemie could be bitter and alone all she wanted. He didn't need to be part of that.

CHAPTER 5

*N*oemie pulled her knit cap down to shield her face as she glanced around furtively at the other shoppers in the party supply store. Once the school day was over, she'd gathered her things, then bolted from work as soon as the last school bus full of students pulled away, intent on beating the after work crowd.

Kissing Springs had one party supply store that carried everything from balloon garland kits, to candy sorted by color for candy bar setups, to toys strictly for the discerning adult over twenty-one.

The shelves and displays containing holiday supplies were scarce, but Noemie paid no attention. For the first time in her life, she was headed for the adult toys, but before she could explore, she wanted to make sure no one she knew was shopping. The last thing she needed was to run into the parent of a student.

She stopped near the Christmas light displays and nodded a greeting toward a young mother, who leaned on a cart that held a sleeping toddler as she perused the mylar balloon selection. Another woman burst into the store and made a beeline for the wedding favors.

She sighed in relief. The store was practically empty.

Noemie looked both ways, like she was crossing the highway and made her way to the adult section of the store, promising herself she'd just take a quick peek. If she found something, she would place her order online.

This was only a fact-finding mission, Noemie decided as she approached the female sex toy aisle. Marveling at the size of the adult section, it threatened to make her dizzy. Who knew Kissing Springs had such a large market for what she considered kink?

Expecting the space to be dark and sleazy, Noemie found the space inviting with well-lit aisles and carefully placed displays.

She picked up a box the size of a cell phone package and gawked. There was an image of the bottom half of a woman's body covered only by a neon green thong. She frowned, her eyes getting bigger as she read each word. *Watermelon gummy flavored edible underwear.* She quickly placed the box back. Not what she was in the market for.

Maybe she should have asked Teresa and Dee, the resident experts for getting themselves off, to tag along. They could help her navigate all the brands and options.

No. She discarded the idea. They'd make a Broadway worthy production out of the whole ordeal. And word would buzz around the teacher's lounge that the new counselor barely knew what a vibrator was, let alone what to do with it.

Curiosity had gotten the best of her after they told her she was uptight and now Noemie was looking for a beginner's kit. Did they sell those?

Her eyes scanned the aisle from top to bottom. So many choices.

Wandering to the end of the aisle, she spied a clearance sign. Never one to pass up a good discount, Noemie started pawing through the racks.

What had Dee mentioned? A bullet? That sounded right. Dee also recommended a brand, but Noemie couldn't recall what it was.

Unlike the regular priced items, the clearance section was a free-for-all with no discernable order to the items. Noemie saw what looked like a beginner's unit behind a larger package. What was that big thing, anyway? Curious, she pulled it from the rack, tilting her head to read the packaging.

She heard someone whistling a tune that sounded vaguely familiar.

Noemie whipped around, searching for an escape route.

She froze as Jameson, the last person on the planet she wanted to run into, rounded the corner with a hand basket full of red sequined items.

He fell silent, stopping short and lifting an eyebrow at her. Annoyance wormed its way through her. Running into Jameson at this exact moment was monumentally worse than colliding with a parent. And his casual manner suggested he came in here all the time. He looked cool and confident while she, on the other hand, was suddenly ready to faint from all the layers she wore.

His eyes shifted toward the item in her hand and Noemie, on impulse, dropped the box like it might explode.

They both looked at the package as it hit the ground with a thud.

Noemie's face got warm as she stared at the Chocolate Thunder Xtra-Large Realistic Look and Feel dildo and realized how this all must look to Jameson.

She should just pack up her apartment now and move to the other side of the planet.

"What are you doing in here?" She blurted the first words that came to mind.

Jameson's lips spread into a knowing smirk. "Remember Brenda from the meeting? She stopped by the gym and asked me to pick up some special-order costumes for the Santa show tonight." He glanced back at the object she'd dropped. "Looks like you've got a busy evening planned."

She knew he would never let her live this down. "That's not...I'm not buying that." She started to explain, then thought better of it. He didn't need to know why she was skulking around the sex toys.

He raised his free hand, palm facing her. "Hey, no judgement here," Jameson said slyly, "but if you get tired of that and want the real thing, let me know."

Noemie sat stunned in the aisle as he resumed his whistling and strolled toward the checkout lane. She wanted to kick the Chocolate Thunder across the store, but instead she picked it up and placed it back on the clearance rack where she found it.

She looked around. As if on cue, the woman with the sleeping toddler appeared, staring at Jameson's retreating figure. "Damn, he was hot," she said in a low voice. "Forget that toy. You should absolutely take him up on his offer."

CHAPTER 6

*T*he week before Christmas, Jameson grunted as he hauled boxes of decorations from the attic storage area in anticipation of his daughter Jordyn's arrival. She told him she'd be home just as soon as she completed her last final exam that afternoon.

He hoped this wouldn't be a visit home where she dropped her stuff off, started a load of laundry and ran off with her friends for the two weeks she was home. He missed hearing about her life and he wanted to be able to see for himself how her first semester of college went.

Jameson dragged the last box into the living room of his modest three-bedroom house. The ranch style home, his first major purchase post-divorce, was his pride and joy.

They'd pick out a tree later that day. Jordyn insisted it wasn't Christmas if the house didn't smell like pine and cinnamon. His suggestion to spray the artificial tree they'd used since she was a toddler with pine scent was met with an eye roll and silence.

Seemed like the women he knew were always rolling

their eyes at him. Noemie had done so a couple of times during their last encounter.

Speaking of which, why had he made that ridiculous statement to Noemie? She looked like she wanted to either slap him or call security after he'd offered to replace the ridiculous toy.

When he rounded the corner and saw her, he was shocked. Noemie was the last person in town he expected to see in the adult toy section, looking at dildos. No, looking wasn't the right word. Noemie had been studying that package like it contained the meaning of life. Like she'd never seen anything like it.

He stopped fussing with the boxes. Jordyn could pick through them and find what she needed.

Now he was curious about Noemie's love life. He could tell she was mortified at being caught, especially by him, but why was she in the adult toy section in the first place? If he had to guess, he was sure it was her first time shopping for such items.

Which meant either she was anticipating a dry spell or she wasn't getting what she needed from her current situation. He scowled, thinking of the new dentist who had his eye on Noemie. If the man's personality was any indication of his bedside manner, Noemie would need reinforcements.

Not that any of this was his business.

"Dad!"

Jameson would have to speculate about Noemie's love life later.

Jordyn burst through the front door and, as she had done since her first days of school, dropped her bags at the door then ran over to embrace her dad.

Jameson resisted the urge to fuss at her about leaving the bags right where he might trip over them, and grabbed her, lifting her off the ground. "Hey Jelly Bean! How did you do on your finals?"

"Dad, I thought we talked about you not calling me Jelly Bean anymore. I'm almost twenty." He set her back on her feet and appraised his only child. She was still small for her age, he worried, but she looked more muscular than she had when he dropped her off. She looked a lot like her mother: deep bronzed skin, big expressive eyes. She stood with her hands on her hips, looking more like a grown woman than he cared to admit.

"You're always going to be my Jelly Bean, no matter how old you get." He tweaked her nose to annoy her then chuckled as she swatted his hand away.

Her eyes rolled skyward as she took in the state of the house. "Dad, it looks like the middle of June in here! You haven't put up any of the Christmas decorations yet."

He shrugged. "I pulled them out, didn't I? I figure you'd want to pick out your color scheme first, then we'd put them up. How were your finals? You got all A's, right? Spending my money wisely?"

"Yes, Dad, I'm spending your money wisely." She balled her fists like she was ready to hit the boxing ring. "I slayed my first Calculus class."

"Good. So how was your first semester? You getting along with your roommates? Any boys I need to go threaten for trying to push up on my baby girl?" He grabbed a large duffle bag that Jordyn had dropped on the floor and grunted. "What do you have in this bag? You trying to get rid of a body?"

Jordyn wrinkled her nose. "Those are dirty. I need to do laundry like right now. And no, even if I was interested in someone, I'm not bringing him home to meet you for a while."

He nodded and changed course, heading for the laundry room in the basement instead of Jordyn's bedroom. Jameson paused at the top of the stairs. "Hmm, I want to meet him. I'll be nice."

She laughed. "No, you won't and no, actually there's no one special enough to bring home yet." She rolled a suitcase toward her room. "What about you? You have no excuse now that I'm out of the house. It's time for you to get out there and find someone to make you happy."

Noemie's face sprang to the forefront of his mind and he swatted the image away. "I don't know, JB. Dating at my age is rough."

"So you'll let me set up an online profile for you?"

Jameson grimaced at the thought and Jordyn grinned at him. "Just kidding, Dad, I know you don't do dating sites." She paused. "You know Mom is getting married again."

It was a statement rather than a question. "Yeah, your grandmother mentioned it. How do you feel about it?"

Jordyn raised her shoulders. "I've only met him twice. I guess he's ok." She strode toward the kitchen. "I don't think she'll keep him around longer than a couple of years. He's kind of passive."

Nodding, Jameson descended the stairs, dropped her duffle in the laundry room and returned to the kitchen. "I assume she'll want you to be a bridesmaid again?"

Full eye roll from Jordyn as she took sandwich makings out of the refrigerator. "Yeah, she'll make me wear the ugliest dress she can find. Can't have the bridesmaids outshine the bride."

"Jordyn..."

"I know, I know. I need to give my mother space to be who she is." She made a face at the whole wheat nine grain bread she found in the pantry but pulled out two slices anyway. "But seriously, this is her third wedding. I don't know why she can't just go to Vegas like everyone else."

He chuckled. "Your mother likes to be the star of the show." He handed her bottles of mustard and mayonnaise, which she slathered on her bread.

"Yeah, she does." She licked the extra mayonnaise off the knife. "Is that why you and Mom split up?"

Jameson was pulling a tomato out of the refrigerator when Jordyn posed the question. He stopped and looked at his daughter, considering his answer. "We were too young. Neither one of us was ready for marriage and parenthood, but I knew that I wanted to raise you. You were mine, and there was no way I was going to let either of our parents take you."

He quickly rinsed and sliced the tomato, handing her a slice for her sandwich. "Your mother and I didn't communicate what we expected from each other in our marriage, but we were too young to know that. That's why we didn't work."

After adding a slice of cheese and lettuce, Jordyn cut the sandwich in half like Jameson used to and placed it on a plate. "That's not what Mom said."

Surprised, Jameson cocked his head. "Really? Do tell."

Jameson had always tried to filter his reactions and thoughts about Jordyn's mother and her eccentricities in front of his daughter. Even though her actions, many times selfish and self-serving, pissed him off, he tried not to let Jordyn see that. He definitely didn't bad mouth her and early on in the relationship, he'd hoped she would extend him the same courtesy. That was foolish on his part.

Before Jordyn could answer, her phone sounded. She dropped the sandwich half after taking a large bite and pulled the phone from her back pocket. "Yara and Izzy want me to go Christmas shopping with them," she said as she tapped out a response. "Can we go get the tree now and I'll tell them I'll meet them afterwards?"

"Sure. Finish your food and we'll get on the road."

Jordyn grabbed him in a quick hug. "Thank you, Daddy, you're the best." She threw a sly look his way. "Oh, also, I might need some money to buy Christmas gifts."

He smiled to himself. She'd held out longer than he thought she would. He was expecting her to hit him up as soon as she dropped her bags off. "Might need?" he teased.

"Ok, definitely need," she said in between bites.

The next evening, a Friday, was Jameson's day to close the gym early. Most of the members who came in on Fridays did so early in the day and since the Santa Revue performed most Fridays, the gym usually emptied out by two and Jamison would close at five. That day was raw and rainy, and the gym hadn't seen a warm body since noon.

Jameson sent the last employee home early and had settled into his office to review ad copy for some upcoming promos he would run after Christmas leading into January, when a knock on the door startled him. He checked the time and realized he'd been sitting with the lights on for almost thirty minutes after closing.

Unless it was one of the Santas, he was going to encourage whoever was at the door to come back first thing in the morning, Jameson grumbled as he made his way to the entrance.

Noemie stood on the other side of the door, waving at him.

His heart raced and the irritation from being interrupted slid away as Jameson unlocked the door for her.

She rushed in, pulling down her hooded raincoat and wiping her feet vigorously on the door mat, talking fast. "Hey, I know you're closed, but I saw the lights on and decided to stop by."

"Noemie, what are you doing out in this weather? Come on back."

"I just left work. Today is the last day before the break and I had a lot to do," she said as she followed him to his office. "So, this is J&J Fitness. I like it. Very modern for little Kissing Springs."

"Thanks." Once they were in the office, Jameson crossed his arms, studying her. She was nervous, almost skittish. "You decided to brave the weather and come see my gym?" he said in disbelief.

"Can we sit?" she said, plopping down into the chair facing his desk.

"Make yourself at home." Jameson watched her eyes dart around the whole space. He wondered what was on her mind.

Noemie picked up a photo of Jordyn from his desk. "Jameson, she's beautiful."

"Thanks. She got her mother's looks."

Noemie frowned slightly, placing the frame back on the desk. Jameson wanted to pull the pat response back as soon as it left his mouth. "You probably don't want to hear anything about her. Jordyn's mother, I mean."

She shrugged. "That's all in the past."

"Yeah, I guess we've all moved on. I just heard she's getting married again."

Nodding, Noemie asked, "Second marriage?"

"Nah, third. I guess she'll keep trying until she gets it

right. At least I'm not paying alimony." Jameson leaned back, tenting his fingers over his chest. "I assume you didn't venture out in the cold to talk about my ex-wife?"

He watched her exhale then blurt, "I want to take you up on your offer."

He frowned, scanning his brain. *Offer? What offer?*

Ah. Now he recalled it. His rusty attempt at flirting.

He forced himself to keep his face neutral. "I was only half serious. I didn't expect...well, it was just something I said."

Her face fell. "Oh my God...ok, forget I said anything. We can talk about..."

"No," he interrupted, "let's talk about this. What is it that you want?" She wasn't going to drop a bomb like that in his lap and just move on to talking about the weather.

Silence.

Jameson watched her try to collect her thoughts. Finally, she spoke. "This is probably the most awkward conversation you've had today, I'm guessing."

He smirked. "Well, it's been a quiet day, so yeah, but you'd be surprised."

She glanced up at him, started to say something, and put the brakes on whatever it was.

Jameson stood then walked around his desk and propped himself against it. "Talk to me, Noemie. I'm not turning you down, just trying to figure out what's up."

"Is it," Noemie cleared her throat, started again. "Is it my weight? I know I was a lot smaller back then, so if that's why you don't...I get it, I mean, you're all..." She motioned at his torso.

He raised his eyebrows. "I'm all what?"

"You know...you're a walking advertisement for a gym.

Like a darker version of The Rock. While I think a full pushup might send me to the emergency room."

Was she kidding? Speechless, Jameson held out a hand to her. After searching his eyes, she took his hand. He pulled her to her feet then led her to the mirrored wall near the weight training area.

He stood behind her, facing the mirror. "What I see when I look at you is a beautiful Black woman with all the curves that hadn't developed yet when she was in college. I see everything I like on a woman...plenty of hips, breasts and the nicest ass in Kissing Springs. Now, if you want to start training so you can eventually do one handed pushups, we can do that, but trust me when I say, you're fine as you are."

Noemie turned toward him. "Are you just saying all this to spare my feelings?"

He chuckled. "I don't say things I don't mean," and he realized this was true for the offer he'd made. "Why do you think I asked for a hug when we were at the meeting?"

Her eyebrows shot up and he nodded. "Yep, not that I wasn't genuinely glad to see you, but it was an excuse to check you out."

She regarded him for a moment, then turned away from the mirror.

"I'm turning forty on Christmas Eve. Because I grew up as a Jehovah's Witness, we never celebrated any holidays, including my birthday. This year I want to do something different for my milestone. I feel like I need to experience life more. I have more regrets than great memories and I want to change that."

He had a million questions, but she continued before he could formulate any of them.

Noemie turned so that she faced him. "You should have been my first...sexual experience."

43

"You were saving yourself for marriage, I thought?" When they were dating that summer, he agreed to respect her wishes, knowing he wasn't ready for a wife; he was working his way through college and could barely support himself. He knew she deserved better. That hadn't stopped him from wanting to be that man for her or from wanting to show her how much she meant to him.

"Yes, but I was also intimidated by you. I never told you this, but I thought I wouldn't measure up to the other girls you'd been with and you'd be disappointed and go find someone with more experience."

He rubbed his face in frustration. "Why didn't you say anything? Noemie, I was crazy about you back then. I would never have been disappointed. I was just happy you wanted to be with me."

"We were too young to know anything about love back then," she said wistfully. "But that's water under the bridge."

She inhaled, then pushed the words out in a rush of breath. "I'm going in eyes wide open now. I want us to have one night together. That is, if you're willing."

He studied her, saw the vulnerability she tried to hide, and it hit him like a baseball to the forehead. That spark she'd ignited in him all those years ago hadn't gone out. Something within her called to something within him.

Jameson stroked his beard. "I'm assuming you want to do this before your birthday?"

She paused. Clearly, she hadn't thought about when this wild night was supposed to happen. "Um, yes?" Her back straightened. "Yes," she said confidently. "A week from today?"

Jameson thought about the following Friday. "I'm pretty sure my daughter will be too busy with her friends to hang out with her old man on a Friday night, but I'll double check. We can have dinner first, go over to Hope's Diner."

Noemie shook her head. "No, you don't have to treat this like an actual date. Besides, I don't want all the tongue wagging when people see us together so you can just come to my house."

His hand went still as his eyes narrowed. "Did you want to sneak me in through the back door?" He didn't mean the question to come out so sharply.

"No, I didn't mean it like that. I just don't want people to assume we're a thing again. I would like my business to stay my business." She crossed her arms, looking up at him.

She didn't want to be seen with him. "Ok, got it. You want me to come in, perform, then be on my way." He was pouting now, lashing out to protect his wounded pride.

"That's not...don't men do this kind of thing all the time? People have one night stands, isn't there some sort of agreement or something?"

"Were you planning to leave some money on the nightstand?" His voice was hard, the question stated through gritted teeth as Jameson attempted to control his anger. "And, yes, people have one night stands all the time. That doesn't mean that I do. I had a daughter to raise, so I didn't have the luxury of running around every night, contrary to what you might believe."

"Who said you were 'running around'?" She did air quotes. "I never said or implied anything like that."

"You came in here like I'm running some kind of escort service." He strode toward his office. "You know what, I don't think this is going to work. Maybe you're better off with one of the toys you were looking at the other day."

Hands on her hips, Noemie followed him into his office

and snatched her jacket. "You're right," she snapped, "this was a bad idea. I'm sorry I wasted your time."

Shrugging her coat back on, she turned back, inches from him. He saw the fire in her eyes and breathed in her now familiar rose scent.

She was about to say something else but froze. Then Noemie's lips parted and before Jameson could stop himself, he'd tugged her close, planting his lips on hers.

CHAPTER 7

*O*nce the shock of her ex-boyfriend kissing her wore off, Noemie knew she should put a stop to the kiss. She should push him away and storm out of his office. She thought for a nanosecond about these things, then all she could think about was the two of them standing in front of the mirror.

I see everything I like on a woman.

She was ready to tell him he had misinterpreted everything she'd said, but the look in his eyes took her speech and sent heat racing through her, stopping at her core, threatening to burn her alive.

He was looking at her like she was the most alluring creature on the planet.

Instead of protesting, she brazenly took his tongue in, then pressed herself against him.

She didn't want to stop kissing him.

She let herself float back in time to the first time she'd kissed Jameson. He'd taken her for burgers and milkshakes where they'd spent the entire meal talking about everything and nothing. He'd teased her about their instructor, an interim staff member filling in for the summer courses, who'd insisted on calling her Naomi.

Once they finished eating, he took her hand. "Hey *Naomi*, come to the park with me. I want to show you something."

"Only if you pronounce my name correctly." She'd felt saucy and flirty, convinced he wouldn't pronounce it right, but secretly hoping he would.

He made a rap out of it. "No-em-mee, the honey with the big brown eyes, looking at me like I'm her prize when all I wanna do is steal her fries," he said, grinning with all the confidence in the world.

She rolled her eyes at his attempt to freestyle. "Not bad, I don't think you're giving the Fresh Prince a run for his money. but you might want to stay in school." She stuck her tongue out, enjoying this down time with him. "What's at the park that you want to show me? I have to be back in an hour for my next class."

"That's plenty of time. Let's go." She noticed he was still holding her hand, and she decided she liked him even though he was a few years older than she.

He made her laugh, and he was a big movie buff, introducing her to Star Wars and taking her to see all the summer's blockbusters.

Once they got to the park, they acted like big kids, twirling on the merry-go-round, which, in hindsight, might not have been the best idea after she'd stuffed herself with a cheeseburger and fries. She'd had him stop the ride when she got lightheaded and slightly nauseated, then when she stepped off the equipment, she'd stumbled.

Jameson caught her, held her, hesitated for a second, then kissed her. It was what she considered her first grown up kiss. The boys she'd gone on dates with in high school, she realized quickly, had nothing on the man seducing her mouth at that moment. She hadn't seen him pop any breath mints, but his kiss was minty, along with the hint of cigarette smoke. That he smoked added to his allure. Her parents considered smoking a cardinal sin.

He'd been gentle at first, then when she'd wanted more, he'd obliged. After they'd come up for air, she'd been practically panting, wondering why it felt like she'd peed her pants a bit.

Now that she was older, she knew what the sensations were. Barely. It had been a while since she'd had the pleasure. And Noemie was now acutely aware that she was playing an extremely dangerous game. She wasn't trying to fall under Jameson's spell again.

She knew better now, didn't she?

Right. If that was the case, she wouldn't be running her fingers over the man's smooth head, wishing this kiss could go on forever.

Noemie pulled away first.

Jameson gave her another scorched glare, then turned toward his desk. "I suppose I should apologize for that."

She sighed. "Please don't." Tugging her jacket down, she looked up at him. "I didn't mean to insult you, Jameson."

How could she express what she needed? How could she tell him she knew she was playing Russian Roulette with her emotions?

Yes, she wanted him. She regretted so many things in her life and this was probably one of her biggest regrets, but she couldn't afford to love him again. That was the reason she didn't want to spend any more time with him than necessary.

"I'm terrible at this," she confessed. "But my awkwardness aside, the last thing I wanted to do was insult you. I wish I could take back this whole evening. I should have kept on walking when I saw you in the window."

"Noemie, why can't we get to know each other again? And let things progress naturally? Are you planning to move back to Charlotte?" he asked suddenly.

"No. At least not anytime soon." She thought about his question. "I guess if something happened to my mother, I might consider leaving, but she's healthy as a horse and the most stubborn person I know. She'll probably outlive us all."

He took her hands in his. "So, if you're not leaving, we can take our time."

Noemie pulled her hands away, making a show of bundling her wool scarf around her neck. "I don't want a relationship right now. I'm still adjusting to my life here and grieving my dad." She gazed up at him, willing him to understand. "I don't have the mental capacity for it."

He nodded, then walked toward the front door, which she knew was her cue to leave.

"Ok, well, it was good seeing you again." He gave her a half smile. She could tell she'd hurt him. Rather than continue to make the unpleasant situation worse, she nodded and hurried out into the cold, rainy night.

Noemie, cozy in her softest pajamas and fuzziest blanket, sat in front of her television, remote in hand, debating.

Did she want to see the tried-and-true classic tearjerker or a new rom com on her streaming service? Maybe she should just watch the rom com. She needed to lighten her mood after seeing Jameson.

Yep, comedy would help. She'd top off her wine glass and sink into the movie so there would be no chance for her to think about his words, or his kiss, or his unreasonable request to take things slowly.

She was on the brink of middle age and he wanted to court her like they were still in college with their whole lives ahead of them.

But honestly, what was her hurry? It wasn't like she needed to get married for the first time. Been there, done that, learned the lessons and vowed never to do it again.

She guessed if she wanted to be a mother, the clock was ticking hard and fast. But she couldn't imagine herself with a newborn. Then, if she did the math, she'd be almost sixty by the time her child graduated from high school, assuming she could get pregnant immediately. She could actually retire with a child in college. The thought made her cringe and gulp her wine. No thanks.

If she were being honest, she'd given up on love after Jameson, and then when she got divorced, she'd given up on having children. She had no desire to raise children by herself and she had sworn off marriage and settled into single life.

There had been a few more dates post-divorce and a long-term relationship that had been born out of mutual friendship and convenience rather than passion, but that fizzled after her dad got sick.

Passion. Pfft. She took another gulp of wine, attempting to wash away the feeling of Jameson's lips on hers. Passion got you in trouble. Passion shredded your heart and shattered your faith in relationships.

She rose to refill her empty wine glass and stopped mid-stride.

Wait a minute. Twice in the same week, she'd been labeled as "uptight."

Had her desire to avoid getting her feelings involved at all costs bled over into all aspects of her life?

Maybe, she shrugged, continuing toward the open bottle of wine on the kitchen counter. She considered pouring another glass and grabbed the entire bottle instead. If she was going to self-reflect, she might as well be good and tipsy during the process.

Along with the wine, Noemie grabbed a notebook and pen from her desk and settled back into the sofa. The movie would have to wait.

Yes, in these last few years, her life consisted mainly of surviving as opposed to actually living and enjoying her time on the planet. And now that she was about to hit the milestone, Noemie wanted to make some bold moves. Well, bold for her, anyway.

Since school was out for the holidays and she had no actual plans for the upcoming week before Christmas, she decided to shake things up and live a little by doing one new thing every day for a week. Opening the notebook to a clean page, she wrote "Saturday" at the top.

An immediate idea hit her as Noemie sipped her wine. She would pamper herself with a facial, massage, and whatever else was on the spa menu on Saturday, then she'd go have a meal at Hope's Diner to top off her day.

Writing the items down, she also made plans for the rest of the week.

Once the bottle of wine was empty, Noemie took it and her glass back to the kitchen, put on some Christmas music and danced excitedly around her apartment.

Her week was full.

"Ms. Saint?"

Noemie stopped mid-stride and turned toward the voice, feeling every bit like an A-List movie star being approached by an eager fan. She had just come from being rubbed, scrubbed, waxed, and polished until she glowed, but she was starving and practically running toward the smell of food.

The new dentist approached, beaming at her. "Remember me? Trevor Hendricks? From the career Fair planning meeting?"

"Of course. How are you, Dr. Hendricks?" She smiled up at him, careful to keep her mouth closed. She didn't want to give him a chance to continue scrutinizing her dental work.

"Call me Trev. I'm good, I've been catching up on paperwork this weekend and stepped out to grab lunch." He motioned toward the door of Hope's Diner, a local eatery. "Were you going in? Can I get the door for you?"

"Oh, yes, I am, thanks." She stood awkwardly for a moment as he stepped in front of her to open the door.

Once they were inside, he turned to her. "Are you expecting anyone else? I did have a couple of questions about the Career Fair. Maybe we can discuss them while we eat?"

Noemie was trapped. She didn't want to be rude and say no, especially since he was donating his time to take part in their event, but she also hadn't planned on a working lunch. "Um, no, it's just me today. Sure, let's get a table."

Trevor looked relieved. He advised the hostess that they wanted a booth and they were told it would be a couple of minutes while they cleared a recently vacated spot near the rear of the restaurant.

Once they settled in at their table, Trevor clasped his fingers together. "This has to be my lucky day. I was going to get my food to go and head back to eat in my office, but I ran into you. I was literally saying to my business partner the other day that I hated I didn't get your business card."

"Yeah, here I am," Noemie said. "Sounds like you conjured me up." She glanced at her watch. "This is a late lunch for you, isn't it?"

"I suppose it is, but I will probably be in the office late today. Everyone is trying to spend their benefits before the end of the year, so we're busy."

Noemie nodded. "How are you enjoying Kissing Springs so far?"

"Oh, I love it! I feel like this is a perfect place for me to settle down. I just need to find a special woman to settle down with." He eyed her, giving her a toothy grin.

Noemie covertly regarded the doctor as she reviewed the menu. Although his hair was thinning, he still had a solid build. She imagined he'd played football at some point, and naturally his teeth were perfect. He wasn't bad looking. He seemed to have a good head on his shoulders along with a thriving dental practice. Overall, he seemed like a good catch and someone with whom she could see herself. But there was no hint of a spark between them, and she suspected why.

He wasn't Jameson.

She couldn't picture the man across from her giving her that look then grabbing her and kissing her like she was the last woman on Earth. She tucked her bottom lip in.

The worst part, she knew, was that she kind of wanted him to do it again.

Trevor closed the menu. "So, what's a pretty woman like you doing eating alone in the middle of the day?"

"Thank you. I just came from the spa and decided I deserved a good meal to top off my day of pampering," she said, placing the menu down. Dessert was in order today, but

Noemie would get it to go and enjoy it at home, possibly in front of the movie she'd abandoned last night.

He nodded. "I get that. I needed to step out myself. Glad I did." He motioned to the server. "You know what you want? I'm getting the special."

The special of the day was Kentucky bourbon glazed pork chops and two sides. Noemie nodded. "Yep, I think I'll get the same thing."

The server placed water glasses and straws on the table, then noted their order.

Once she was gone, Trevor put a hand under his chin, staring at Noemie. "You look great, by the way, but I'm sure you hear that all the time."

She thanked him again as he continued to stare.

She almost wished they were talking about teeth whitening again. "So. Where was home before you moved here to Kissing Springs?"

"Louisville. I've got an office there as well, but once I saw how this town is growing, I wanted to get in while the real estate is still affordable." Trevor said, "And I figured with all these bachelorette parties coming here, maybe I can snag a bride."

Noemie nodded.

"So, the big bald dude, from the meeting, he's a stripper?" Trev asked suddenly.

Noemie frowned, then realized he was referring to Jameson. She supposed that was a fair assumption to make. Jameson certainly had the body for it, but she couldn't picture him dancing naked for a crowd of strangers.

Wait, did they get naked at those shows? "No, the guys that do the shows work out at his fitness center."

"Ok." Trevor watched her. "You dating him?"

She almost snorted. "No." At this point, she didn't know if

they were even friends after her botched attempt to proposition him.

He laid his arms on the table. "Hmm, he seemed to mark his territory. So, what if I wanted to take you to dinner?"

A server rushed over with their plates. Noemie smiled at the server, grateful for the interruption.

"Trevor, I appreciate the offer, but I lost my father earlier this year and moved back here to Kissing Springs. I'm not ready to think about any of that right now. I hope you understand."

Pausing before digging into his food, Trevor said, "Oh, I didn't know. I'm sorry for your loss."

She thanked him and an awkward silence fell over the table as they both concentrated on their meals.

Noemie realized being pampered worked up an appetite, as she attacked the tender chops, mashed potatoes, and green beans. The well-prepared food lived up to its promise of comfort, and her mood lightened.

She was just about to ask Trevor more about his time in Louisville when a familiar silhouette stepped into the diner, greeting several of the other patrons.

Carla Mitchell was a petite woman with olive skin and rich brown eyes that conveyed her every emotion. Her eyes widened when she caught Noemie's eye and she made a beeline for their booth.

"Noemie! I was wondering when we might run into each other. You've been here for months and I've missed you each time I visit your mother."

Noemie stood and embraced Jameson's mother warmly. She'd always liked the woman's mother hen ways, so different from her own mother. "Hey, Mrs. Mitchell, I've been busy adjusting to my new job and settling Dad's affairs."

Carla put a hand to her heart. "Oh, I'm sure. And please

call me Carla. We all miss your dad down at the community center." She seemed to notice Trevor for the first time. "Well, Dr. Hendricks, this is a pleasant surprise."

Carla raised a perfectly arched eyebrow at Noemie before turning back to Trevor. "We never see you out and about these days."

Trevor chuckled. "I'm usually too busy for lunch, but I decided to step out for a quick bite and ran into Ms. Saint. I'm going to take part in the career fair."

Noemie nodded to corroborate the story, as if Carla caught her doing something she had no business doing.

"Right, well, don't let me keep you both," she put a hand on Noemie's arm. "I'm helping out at the fitness center most mornings; you should stop by so we can have lunch."

"Ok, I'd like that."

"Good! I'll get your number from Jameson. Happy holidays, Dr. Hendricks!" With that, Carla turned and joined her friends at their table.

Noemie watched the woman walk away, noting that Jameson and his mother had the same gait. And, now that she thought about it, the same expressive dark brown eyes. She was sure the woman would mention seeing her out with Trevor, and she wondered what his reaction would be.

CHAPTER 8

Sunday morning, Jameson held a beverage container with two coffees in one hand as he fumbled with the keys to open the fitness center in the other. He dropped the keys and swore, staring at them on the cold concrete sidewalk. Bending to pick them up, his mother appeared on the other side of the door and pushed it open so he could enter. Would have been nice if she had gotten there a few seconds earlier, he groused.

"You're running late this morning," she said, taking the container and placing it on the front desk.

"Yeah, I had to drop a package off at the post office." He motioned at the cup nearest him. "That's yours. Anything going on today?"

"Nope. I made cookies for the town's first cookie exchange," she answered, sipping her coffee.

"Oh ok," he said, absently thinking about all the items on his to do list. He nodded, raising the lidded cup to his lips.

Jameson paused, eyebrows raised. His mother was still staring at him, looking like she had much to say.

"You know I saw Noemie at the diner yesterday with the new dentist," she said finally. "They looked awfully cozy."

He tried to keep his tone casual. "Nope, I didn't know that."

Sighing, he waited. Even though he towered over his mother, she had this way of making him feel like he was still a little boy.

He knew a lecture was coming when she put her coffee down with a thud. "So, you're going to let him sweep her off her feet right under your nose? Did you ask her out for coffee like I suggested?"

"Ma, she's still mourning, it's complicated." He wasn't about to tell his mother about their last conversation, how she only wanted one night.

"Mm-hmm, he said they ran into each other in front of the diner, but I wouldn't be surprised to find out he was waiting for her to show up. Something about that Trevor Hendricks...he rubs me the wrong way."

As long as he wasn't rubbing Noemie. Jameson though the man was odd when he met him too, standing too close to Noemie at the career fair.

"Jameson David Mitchell. You've been pining for that woman all these years and now that she's back in town to stay, and single, no doubt, you're standing here with excuses?" She huffed, making her way to the front desk and turning on the laptop. "Good thing I have a Plan B."

"What did you say? What's going on, Ma?" *Yep, his mother was up to something.* "And I'm not pining."

"Nothing, don't worry about it. One of the rowing machines needs to be serviced, you want me to call it in?"

"Yeah, thanks." He studied her closely. "You're not up to anything, right?"

"I'm trying to make sure we provide a world class fitness

experience for the members, which means I have work to do, as I assume you do, too."

Some days he wasn't sure who was running the business. "Fine, I'll be in my office."

An hour later, several gym members were getting their workouts in and a yoga class was in full swing when Noemie breezed in. Jameson had been thinking about his mother's words and wondering how much he needed to worry about Mr. Dental Floss when he saw her walk in and greet his mother.

When she merely waved at him and collected a large bag from his mother, he frowned. Clearly Ma was expecting her.

He walked out to greet her, bracing himself for a frosty reception, recalling the last time she came in. But he reminded himself, there was one good memory from her last visit. She'd kissed him back when he'd reached for her, but he didn't need to think about that right now.

"Good morning, Noemie, what brings you in today?"

She turned to him, her eyes resting briefly on his mouth before she met his eyes. "Carla asked me to stop by and pick up a donation for the toy drive and we're going to help setup for the cookie exchange later on."

Jameson raised an eyebrow at his mother. Why hadn't she mentioned Noemie was stopping by? "Oh ok."

She stood, wringing her hands. "Noemie, I've got to get a service request done for one of the machines. I don't think I can step out right now."

Jameson started to tell her that she could go, he'd handle things when she raised her palms like she'd had an epiphany. "Jameson, you go in my place. Help her get that bag in her car, please, son."

Really, Ma? He stared at her in wonder.

"Oh, Carla, no, I'm sure he's busy." Noemie swung her gaze between the two of them. "Aren't you?"

He did have plenty of work to do. But an image of Hendricks cozying up to Noemie tasting her cookies popped into his head. *Nope.* "Actually, I can probably lend a hand for a couple of hours."

"Perfect!" His mother placed a hand on her chest like he'd performed a miracle. "I'll hold things down here. You go help out. I'll call you if I need you. Actually, I'm gonna wake up Jordyn and have her come keep me company."

Covering his mouth with his hand to keep from commenting on his mother's Oscar-worthy performance, Jameson motioned to the bag in Noemie's hand. "I can take that, you ready?"

Once they were outside alone walking toward Noemie's car, she smirked. "Why do I get the feeling we've just been set up?"

"Yep. Greatest dramatic performance since Hattie McDaniel in Gone with the Wind," he muttered.

Noemie threw her head back in laughter. "Your mother is something else."

She pressed her key fob to unlock the doors of her SUV and Jameson slid into the passenger seat. The community center was a quick drive from the center of town.

Watching her, Jameson decided she needed to laugh more. The joy on her face made his mother's meddling worthwhile.

"What?" she said, starting the car. "What's wrong?"

"Nothing at all. Nice to see you enjoying the moment, even though I want to crawl under a rock from embarrassment."

"You? I can't imagine that sweet woman ever embarrassing you." She nudged him with her shoulder as they hauled in the bags of cookies and toys.

"Yeah, today was nothing. When I got into trouble at school, she'd come in and sit in my classes, giving me the evil eye the whole class." He imitated his mother's glare.

"No, she didn't! Are you serious?"

"Yes, I am. Ask her next time you see her."

The cookie exchange was being held in the arts and crafts room where several tables were set up around the perimeter of the room. Noemie led Jameson to the room and he opened the door for them.

Teresa Lee rushed over to them. "Saint! Thank you for coming! And bringing cookies!"

"Hey Teresa, I brought brownies as well, I didn't know if anyone might want them." Placing the bags on the nearest table, Noemie gave Teresa a quick hug.

"Cookies, brownies, it'll all get eaten I'm sure," she said, then turned to Jameson. "Hey Jameson! I'm surprised to see you here. I thought Carla was coming?"

He shrugged. "She shooed me out of my own building, claiming she's got too much work to do."

Teresa glanced at him then at Noemie and raised an eyebrow. "I see."

Those two words spoke volumes and Jameson knew that this outing with Noemie might as well be broadcast on the evening news. Everyone in town would be speculating about them by dinner.

He crossed his arms. "What do you need me to do?"

Teresa sighed. "Saint, the last thing you probably want to do today is supervise kids but we desperately need two people to man the gingerbread house building station."

"That actually sounds like fun. Looks like we're on gingerbread duty," Noemie smiled at him and the prospect of making houses out of candy with her and a bunch of boisterous children did sound like fun.

They nodded and Teresa walked them to an area with tables and a stack of gingerbread kits. She pointed at the kits. "Maybe use one kit as the demo to show the kids how it's supposed to look?"

The woman rushed off after hearing her name, leaving them alone to set up their workspace. Jameson had never done this activity with his daughter but how hard could it be? He picked up a kit. Basic, not fancy. They could do this.

Noemie looked like she'd been asked to build the Eiffel Tower. "Maybe I spoke too soon. You've done this before, right? I have no clue."

Right. She hadn't grown up celebrating Christmas. "No, my daughter was never into building these things but it looks fairly straightforward."

They set the kits out along with wet towelettes and extra frosting and candy. The exchange was scheduled to start in another hour.

Noemie popped a chocolate kiss in her mouth and handed two to Jameson. "Thanks for helping. I'm sure you were actually busy today."

"There are always things I could be doing but my mother and Jordyn should be able to handle the place for a couple of hours. Sometimes I feel like it's Ma's gym and I just work there."

She grabbed his hand. "What you've done with the place is amazing; you should be proud. I can tell she's proud of you."

He stared at their hands together for a moment then raised his eyes to hers. He wanted to kiss her so badly it hurt. "Are you?" he asked softly.

"Yes, of course. I've always had faith you would do whatever you set your mind to." She rubbed her thumb against his hand. "And I apologize again for the other day. I want us to be friends."

He'd promised he wouldn't push. He would let things progress in their own time, but the question escaped before he could catch it. "Noemie, is that all you want us to be?"

Another volunteer hurried over with her arms full of additional gingerbread kits. "More donations. I think we'll have plenty for any of the kids who want to participate." She set the kits on the table. "Kids should show up any minute now." With that, she was off again.

Jameson watched her leave then turned back to Noemie, ready to pick up their conversation but the look on her face stopped him. She was staring at him with regret, which meant she did only want to be friends.

He ran a hand over his face. *Fine.* They would hash this out at some point.

Two fitness center members approached with their children in tow. He greeted them and got them set up with gingerbread house kits.

As more parents stopped by, he and Noemie passed out the kits and got them started. Once the seats were all taken, they worked together to demonstrate how the house was supposed to look.

He took out the pieces of gingerbread and set them out while Noemie prepped the frosting tube. Handing her the first wall of the house, their hands brushed. The touch sent a warm current through his body and he fought the urge to take her hand. She glanced at him, something he couldn't quite name flashing in her eyes before she turned to answer a question from one of the kids.

She wasn't immune to him. Good to know he wasn't the only one struggling.

Together, they managed to build the house and decorate it with the candy in the kit. The kids cheered, eager to build their own houses. Noemie walked around to help and Jameson noted she was a natural with the children.

He wondered if she wanted kids of her own. Could he raise another child or two at this stage in his life? He shrugged. Not a terrible idea. Since he already had a daughter, a son would be nice. Jordyn would probably freak out at becoming a big sister but she'd adjust.

He envisioned a pregnant Noemie letting him feel his son's kicks. A sense of contentment filled him, sealing the deal. Yeah, if she wanted a baby after they got married, he was on board.

Jameson caught himself. Not an hour ago, she'd pushed him into the friend zone and here he was picking out baby names.

She touched his arm to get his attention, concern on her face. "Hey, Jameson, could you get the extra frosting from that bag behind you?"

"Sure, let me grab it." Realizing he was scowling, Jameson bent to fish the frosting out of the bag.

He handed the tube to her. "I'll be back, you ok by yourself for a few minutes?"

"Yep, we're good," she peered at him. "You ok?"

He waved his hand. "I'm fine. Be right back." He needed to step away for a minute and clear his head.

CHAPTER 9

$\mathcal{N}$oemie watched Jameson hurry out of the arts and crafts room like he had urgent business to take care of. He was acting strangely. Should she go after him?

Teresa strode over, placing a red plastic cup in Noemie's hand. "A little Christmas cheer for you."

Noemie sipped the concoction, then coughed. "What is this? I thought it was eggnog?"

"There's a little egg in it. Mostly nog though." She wiggled her eyebrows. "It's my secret recipe." She leaned in, grasping Noemie's arm. "So…I thought you didn't have a boy toy. Not that Jameson is anyone's boy."

"He's not my boy toy, we're just…friends." Noemie placed the cup on the table. For some reason, the words didn't sit well with her, even though she'd been the one to define their relationship.

"Friends? Saint, he's a good man and he's single. I hear he never got over his first love, someone he met in college way back when..." she trailed off, her brows furrowed in thought.

Teresa's eyes widened. "Wait a minute! Are you The One that Got Away? But you went to Spelman, right?"

Noemie, ignoring Teresa's questions, turned to watch the door. Jameson hadn't made it back to their table and was talking to a woman she recognized as the mother of one of her students. The woman was standing too close to him for comfort, grinning and tossing her obviously fake ponytail in his direction.

Maybe she couldn't handle being just his friend. She was ready to grab the woman by the faux tail and drag her from the building.

Teresa tsked beside her. "If that woman spent half as much time helping her kids with their homework as she did chasing after the Santas, they wouldn't be failing." She tapped Noemie's arm. "Don't worry about her. Do you and Jameson have history?"

Noemie closed her eyes. *History* didn't begin to cover what she'd felt for him back then.

"Oh, shi... I mean, sugar, it is you!" Teresa exclaimed.

Before Teresa could interrogate her further, Noemie felt a small hand tugging on the hem of her sweater. "Ms. Saint," a small boy of about seven asked, his tone earnest. "Can you help me hold up my walls?" he pointed at the pile of ginger-bread at his table.

She smiled down at him, bending so that she was eye level with him. He had on a name tag that identified him as Liam. "Of course, Liam, let's put it back together."

The boy led her to his table as Teresa mouthed, "We'll talk about this later." and hurried back to the beverage table.

Noemie was elbow deep in frosting and gingerbread, holding the foundation of the house together while the owner took off to get more cookies when Jameson returned. He cocked an eyebrow at her when he approached her table. "You decided to do another house without me?"

"No, this is Liam's house and he's making a cookie run." She shifted uncomfortably. "Is it sturdy enough to leave it so it can dry? I need to find the ladies room."

He rubbed his chin, surveying the house. "Yeah, let's switch places, I'll take a look." He placed his large hands over hers, holding the walls of Liam's house together.

In that moment, Noemie breathed in his scent, a woodsy after shave and fresh laundry combination, as each nerve ending in her body reacted to his touch and his voice in her ear.

"House looks good, I got it." He was close enough that if she leaned over just a bit, she could give in to her body and place her lips on his, pull him in right here in the open, give the town gossips a headline story to run with.

Jameson seemed to read her mind. He was staring at her, desire in his eyes, silently daring her to make the first move.

Despite every cell in her body telling her to go for it, show him that she wanted more than his friendship, she stood up, moving out of his space, and the moment passed.

Later, as they were cleaning up, marveling at the sheer amount of frosting and candy everywhere they turned, Teresa paused to drop off a colorful bag for each of them. "Thank you both for your help today!"

She fanned herself, winking at Noemie. "Goodness, it's hot in here...anyway, the gingerbread houses were a hit! I went around and snagged a few of the best cookies for you both. We're heading out in a few but the security guards will lock up after you leave. Saint, we'll have to do lunch soon."

Noemie knew what that meant. Teresa was going to want details on Jameson.

Once Teresa was gone, Noemie tore the sticker off the bag, inhaling the scent of sugar, frosting, chocolate and vanilla. She knew she shouldn't, but she was starving.

"Ooh, I hoped Mrs. Kerrigan would bring these." She pulled out a red velvet sandwich cookie and took a bite, rolling her eyes toward the heavens. "You have to try this, one of the moms brought them in for the staff and they will bless your entire soul," she said, her mouth full. She held out the cookie for him to try.

Jameson chuckled, breaking off a bite sized piece. "I'm surprised you're sharing if they're that good." He tasted the cookie and nodded in appreciation.

She finished the cookie, wishing she had milk to wash it down when she looked up and caught Jameson smirking at her. "I know, I know, my manners are atrocious but I'm starving."

"No, come here, you've got a little of the cream cheese filling on your face."

She stepped closer, rubbing at her face. Noemie was certain she had a small mirror in her purse which was buried in one of the boxes they needed to load into her car.

"Wrong side, I'll get it." With that, he licked the corner of her mouth with the faintest touch before capturing her lips in a slow, intense kiss that she felt all the way to her toes. She dropped the bag at some point, leaving her hands free to rub the freshly trimmed beard on his cheeks.

This was bliss, she thought, as his mouth explored hers. He tasted like the cookie they just shared. Sweet, sensual, familiar. Her thighs parted slightly, her body sending signals she wouldn't voice. She wanted him.

Yes, the naggy little voice in the back of her mind said, *but you wanted him that summer, almost gave in and look where that got you? Broken hearted and alone, grabbing the first man who looked your way and marrying him.*

The voice might as well have dumped a bucket of ice on her head. She tensed, pulled away and immediately regretted it.

Jameson stepped back, folding his arms across his chest. "Oh, that's right. You don't want everyone in your business. Or," he stroked his chin, "it's that you don't want to be seen with me."

Noemie stiffened. Was he spoiling for a fight tonight? "What? I never said I don't want to be seen with you."

"You might as well have. You don't want to have dinner with me in a public place." Jameson shoved the gingerbread house supplies into a large box on the floor. "But I guess it's ok to be seen out to lunch with the corny dentist."

Noemie frowned. "That lunch wasn't planned. I fully intended to eat by myself but he asked if he could talk to me about the career fair and I said ok." She pushed her arms together, mirroring his stance. "I don't know why you're making such a big deal out of it. That lunch has nothing to do with us."

"You want to know why that lunch was a big deal to me? Because I thought this was going to be our second chance. I know we can't just pick up where we left off twenty years ago, but I wanted us to get to know each other. But joke's on me, you only want sex." They faced each other, the cookies forgotten.

She was going to lay her cards on the table. Well, not all of her cards. She couldn't tell him about the reasons she wanted to sleep with him. "The last time I fell for you, I got my heart broken. I had to hear from your pregnant girlfriend that you had a baby on the way. I was blindsided and it took me a long time to get over that. So, I'm cautious now and I'd appreciate it if the whole town isn't involved in our relationship."

"Oh, you're cautious now so you just want to be fuck buddies? Is that it?"

Noemie's mouth dropped. "I would *never* use that awful word to describe us. Never."

Jameson picked up the box. "Why not? That's what it is to you. I'm going to put this box in your car then I'm heading home."

Before she could respond, he stomped toward the exit.

"Wait, don't you need a ride to your car?" Noemie called, grabbing the cookie bags and shoving them in her purse. She was going to need them after tonight.

"No. Don't worry about it."

They walked out of the building toward Noemie's car in silence. Once they reached the car, she pointed the key fob at it to open the trunk. She watched him shove the box in. "You might as well let me take you back to the gym so you can get your car."

He closed the trunk with more force than needed and Noemie winced. "I said don't worry about it. Go home, Noemie."

Fine. She started toward the driver's side of the car, shaking her head in frustration. He was so pigheaded.

Noemie stopped, turned back to Jameson. "If you don't get in the car, I swear I'm calling your mother."

He raised his gaze toward her. "Is that supposed to be a threat?"

"It is a threat! Get in the car," she snapped then remembered her manners. "Please."

He glowered while he appeared to weigh his options.

She dug her phone out of her purse and held it up.

Jameson swore.

She tapped the phone's screen.

He opened the door, folded himself into the passenger seat and snatched the seat belt across his chest.

"Thank you." She got in, dropped the phone in the cup holder and put her seat belt on as well.

They rode in silence for a mile before Jameson spoke. "I didn't intentionally set out to deceive you back then. Vanessa, Jordyn's mother, and I were off and on for two years until we broke up for good, so I thought, a few months before I met you." He ran a hand over his head. "Once she told me she was pregnant, we talked about giving the baby up for adoption. I honestly thought that we were in agreement that we were too young to be parents. Next thing I know, she's running around town telling people we're having a baby."

He studied his hands. "I was ashamed. I couldn't face you; I didn't know how to tell you. She gloated that she 'set you straight' and I didn't do anything."

They were both so young back then. But regardless of her age, Noemie's feelings for Jameson were real and nothing she'd felt for any man, her ex-husband included, since. She kept her eyes on the road.

"I loved you, Noemie. And not contacting you before you went back to school was the biggest regret of my life."

Noemie's heart thumped loudly in her chest. He was confessing, why couldn't she? Too soon. She would admit to one thing. "I loved you too."

"I'm sorry for not reaching out. Especially when you dad died. There were so many times I wanted to find your number, friend you on Facebook and ask how you were doing but I didn't and now that you're here, seems like all we do is butt heads."

When she pulled up to the gym, the place was dark. Jameson's lone pickup truck sat in the parking lot. Noemie parked next to it and cut the engine.

"Maybe we can start over?" she said, turning to look at him. His normal energetic demeanor was gone, he was reliving the past she could tell and he was caving to the weight of it. "Let's get to know one another again, as friends?"

He nodded, taking her hand in his. "Yeah, that's what I want, for us to start over."

He rubbed his thumb over her knuckles. Noemie found his touch both soothing and arousing. She wanted him to rub his hands all over her bare skin.

The inner nag popped up on her shoulder like a cartoon devil. *You just told the man you wanted to be friends. Friends don't fantasize about their friends' hands stroking their lady gardens.*

He cleared his throat. "I do have one request. While we're getting to know each other again, could we keep Mr. Dental Floss out of the picture?"

Noemie tucked her lips in to hold back a chuckle. She shouldn't encourage him. "I don't know Trevor well enough to consider him a friend. And why do you call him that?"

"I have another name for him that's not so nice. So around you, I call him Mr. Dental Floss."

"I'm not even going to ask," she said finally.

"That's for the best." He released her hand, preparing to exit the car. "Thank you for tonight. I wanted you to know how I...well, I just wanted you to know."

Noemie wanted to hug him, tell him all was forgiven but she wasn't there yet. While his confession provided some closure, she couldn't ignore the pain his actions had caused.

She nodded as he got out of the car, more conflicted than ever. At least they hadn't thrown sex into the equation but she wasn't sure how long that would last.

73

CHAPTER 10

"W ho knows why exercise is good for your body?" Jameson asked the sea of elementary school children sitting on mats in the class studio at his gym.

The children looked at each other and one girl with lopsided pigtails pushed her hand up then yelled. "Because so you won't get a big butt when you have kids."

The kids laughed and Jameson stifled a grin. Those words had to be the echo of some frazzled mother.

"Not quite. We exercise so our bodies build muscles which help our bodies function better. We get strong when we exercise." He held up a flexed bicep. "See, this is a strong muscle. This means I can lift heavy things."

"Can you lift a car?" a boy in the front with glasses asked.

"He can't lift a whole car," the boy next to him scoffed. "That's stupid."

"We don't use that word here, Tyler. And we encourage each other to ask questions if we don't know something, right?"

The kids nodded back at him.

"No, a car weighs thousands of pounds so I don't try to lift those. I can lift any of those weights over there." He pointed at the free weight display stocked with dumbbells.

He scanned the kids' expectant faces. They were so young. Their lives should be carefree but most were here because their working parents couldn't afford child care and had nowhere else to take them.

For a few children sitting in front of him, the box lunch he would serve would be their only meal that day.

"Ok!" He clapped his hands together. "Who's ready to do our animal stretches?"

Screaming, the kids popped up from their seated positions, hands waving. They loved animal stretches.

Jameson placed the whistle around his neck in his mouth and blew one quick breath into it.

The kids stood at attention. "Claws out! Feet up! Now stomp like a T-Rex! And don't forget to GROWL!!"

A dozen little dinosaurs growled, stomping around the gym, arms in front of their chests.

He blew the whistle again after a few minutes. "Stop! Now we transform into what?"

"Eagles!" The class screamed.

Soon they had all spread their arms as wings and were flying.

Jameson was about to blow the whistle again when he glanced toward the door.

He assumed it was one of the trainers stepping in to take over.

His main physical fitness trainer who usually worked with the kids called in sick that morning, so he had to cover the day camp session. He didn't mind. He liked working with the kids, even though he'd be exhausted by the time they ended for the day.

Jameson's eyebrows shot up as Noemie's head poked through. This was a surprise. She smiled tentatively at him, wiggling her fingers in a quick wave.

Turning his attention back to the kids, he blew the whistle longer this time. "Ok! Five minute free style! Be whatever animal you want to be, but don't eat the other animals!"

The kids screeched and took off running like they had been set loose from cages.

Jameson motioned Noemie in the room.

As she strode toward him, barely avoiding what he assumed was a runaway elephant, Jameson worked to keep his face passive. They were supposed to be friends and he didn't want to get caught giving her the eye.

"Hey, your mother said it was ok for me to come in here. I didn't mean to interrupt," she said, looking around.

"Don't worry about it. We're about to break for lunch in a few minutes." Jameson took in everything about her. The boatneck black top, long wool skirt and riding boots. The hair slicked back into a low bun at the nape of her neck that he wanted to run his fingers through. The kissable berry lips.

She looked like she was on her way to an important affair. Maybe the dentist was taking her to lunch again. That thought made him scowl.

Out of nowhere, a burning desire to take her dancing hit him. He wanted to hold her close and lead her around a dance floor. Instead, he clasped his hands behind his back. "This is a surprise. What brings you by today?"

"You're great with the kids," she responded. "They love you." She sounded surprised.

"Well, I do feed them, that might be one reason." His tone

was dry. "But I love hanging out with them and letting them use their imagination."

He turned his head toward two kids tussling. "Hey, Jaylin, Zander, break it up! Be polite animals."

He watched as the two boys separated reluctantly then turned his focus back to Noemie. "Most times I do, anyway. Where are you off to?"

She motioned toward the front. "I'm going shopping for more age-appropriate items."

Jameson frowned, intent on asking her what that meant when the door opened again and a tall male trainer with a J&J Fitness golf shirt hurried in. "Hey, Mr. Jay, sorry I'm late. Want me to take over from here?"

The man glanced at Noemie. "Sorry for interrupting."

"Adam, this is Ms. Saint. Adam's one of our fitness trainers."

The two exchanged greetings.

Jameson motioned toward the chaos. "Yeah, Adam, give them a few more minutes, then they can go have their lunches."

Adam nodded, ambling off to corral the children.

"Let's go to my office where it's quiet," he said, leading her out of the class studio.

Once they were in his office, he opted to prop himself against his desk rather than sit in his chair. The chair felt too formal.

"Age-appropriate clothing, what exactly does that mean?"

Noemie looked down at her clothing. "My wardrobe needs a refresh. And I need to buy things that a forty-year-old woman should have, like a nice cocktail dress."

"Are you going somewhere special?" Jameson asked, his mind immediately conjuring an image of the dentist spinning Noemie in a little black dress around a dance floor. He ran a frustrated hand over his beard. This woman had him in knots.

"No, but I'm trying to live my best life, as they say, so I'll have it if I need it." She played with a bangle on her wrist then sighed. "I have a favor to ask, are you free for dinner tonight?"

"Does this favor involve tools, or a ladder, or a moving truck?"

She frowned slightly. "No, not at all."

He waited a few seconds to see if she would elaborate. "Ok, then, sure, we can have dinner. Where do you want to go?"

"I was planning to cook for you, so we'd be at my place. Does that work?" Noemie was twisting the bangle like she meant to unscrew it from her wrist. The favor she wanted had to be huge. "And if tonight isn't good, I understand. I know your daughter is in town. Do you have plans with her?"

He crossed his arms. "Spending time with her family is pretty low on Jordyn's list right now," he said, then held up a finger. "But...I'm in luck. She's penciled me in for tomorrow. I'm taking her shopping for a new Ipad."

Noemie gave him a sympathetic smile which sent his heart racing. How was it possible that Noemie was even more beautiful now than she was when he'd first laid eyes on her? If he wasn't careful...

"Yeah, my first time back from Spelman, I had no time for my parents either. I treated them like they were my minions. But once the novelty of being back home from school wears off, she'll want to spend more time with you. I'm sure she's a Daddy's girl like I was."

He nodded. "I hope so. For now, I guess I'll take what I can get." Jameson rubbed his chin. "That goes for you, too.

I'm not one to turn down a good home cooked meal. What time do you want me to come over and what can I bring?"

"A bottle of wine is fine."

The phone in front of him rang loudly, shattering the connection between them. Jameson checked the display. "Hey, Ma, what's up?"

"There's a man out here asking for you. Said he's a business associate of Dalton's."

Jameson bobbed his head, recalling that Dalton, the owner of Derby Nights, had mentioned the visit during one of their poker nights. "Yeah, his name is Dec, I think. I'll be out in a sec."

He hung up, walking over to hold the door for Noemie. "I'll see you tonight."

"Food will be ready at seven. I'll text you my address." She rose, arched her back in a stretching motion, causing her breasts to thrust forward. Jameson reluctantly pulled his gaze away before his tongue hit the ground.

He met her eyes and cleared his throat. "Ok," he managed to say before she stepped out of the door.

Stepping out of his office, he saw that his mother was showing a tall, muscular African-American in his early thirties around the gym. Jameson strode over and introduced himself, taking over the tour from her.

The man gripped Jameson's hand earnestly. "I'm Dec Dorsey...nice spot you got here."

"Thanks, man. Dalton said you're from Nashville, right?"

"Yeah, and if you ever think about expanding into other cities, let me know. My guys would love a place like this for their workouts."

Jameson tilted his head. He hadn't considered expansion yet. "I'll think about that. In the meantime, feel free to drop in and workout while you're in town."

Dec nodded, thanking him.

Jameson clapped the younger man on the back and returned to his office, his mind replaying Noemie's invitation. He was intrigued to see what favor she needed but he was getting a free meal out of it, how bad could it be?

Jameson stood at the door of Noemie's apartment, nervous like they were sixteen and headed to their prom. He grimaced. Why was he so on edge? He'd known this woman for twenty years, he could be cool about the whole thing, couldn't he?

No. Tonight was different, he sensed. They were at a crossroads and tonight would decide which road they took. He knew which road he wanted them to take. Now that Noemie was back in Kissing Springs for good, it was their time. They were both single and living in the same town for a reason. They had unfinished business.

He straightened his wool coat, wishing he had access to a mirror. He'd debated on wearing a tie but Jordyn told him that was way too formal, so he opted to wear a navy sweater and slacks.

"Just be yourself, Dad. If she doesn't like who you are, she's not worth your time," she said, looking like him when he lectured her. She was hosting Christmas movie night for her friends which meant he wouldn't worry about her coming home at odd hours.

She'd also asked him if he had condoms, which was as uncomfortable a moment as he'd probably ever had with his daughter. Mortified didn't begin to explain his reaction. He'd tersely nodded and hurried out of the house. He sighed. He guessed he'd taught her well.

He shifted the bouquet of red roses, white lilies, and carnations under his arm and rang the doorbell. *Here we go.* The jitters in his stomach flared up as he waited for her to answer the door.

Noemie opened the door, releasing the warmth of the apartment and the pungent onion and spices from the meal to hit Jameson.

Jameson started to speak but couldn't. Whenever he heard someone describe something as "breathtaking" he immediately assumed they were exaggerating, but at this moment that was the only term that came to mind. Noemie looked radiant. Her hair was styled so that it fell in soft waves and she was wearing a red dress with a deep V that showed off all of her curves.

Breathtaking.

This was going to be a long night if she wanted him to act like they were just friends. He groaned inwardly. Her berry-stained lips were begging to be kissed, as was the spot at her throat where he could see her pulse quicken.

She did her share of gawking, he noticed. "Hey, you look beautiful, as always," he said finally.

"Thank you, so do you. Well, not beautiful, of course… you look handsome and I'm babbling," She stepped aside so he could enter. "Sorry, come in."

He chuckled at her, glad it wasn't just his nerves getting the best of him. She was nervous too.

"These are for you. And the wine you asked for." He handed her the flowers and the bottle.

"Thank you, these are lovely." She inhaled the flowers. "I'll put these in a vase. Dinner's almost ready but I need to check on it so make yourself at home." With that, she dashed into the kitchen.

"The food smells great," he called out, taking in the space.

Jameson needed to focus on something other than how much he wanted to peel Noemie's fiery red dress off of her, he strolled around, observing.

He could tell by the scale of her furniture that her place in Charlotte was probably much larger than the modest apartment she was in now. He wondered about her life in Charlotte. He wasn't even sure what she'd done for work there. He'd ask over dinner. Another thing to talk about that would keep him focused. They were going to take things slow, he reminded himself. The only seducing he should be doing tonight would be mental.

He shrugged. He'd try, but no promises.

Above the low entertainment stand and flat screen television were floating shelves filled with photos. Jameson studied the pictures of Noemie with her family. There was a recent shot of her with her dad sitting in lounge chairs, a beach at sunset in the background.

"Where was your mom in this picture of you and your dad? And what beach is that?" he called into the kitchen.

"That's the Outer Banks. And my mom was taking the pictures. She's a photography buff so she's the one behind the camera in a lot of my photos," she called out. "She hates the way we take them."

Jameson smiled. "You look like you were having a good time."

He moved on to another picture where Noemie was standing in cap and gown. Graduation day. But he knew it wasn't her Spelman graduation. She had on the more elaborate garb for master's graduates. Jameson wondered if his lack of degrees would be a problem for her. He'd managed to scrape by and get an associate's degree but had no interest in going any further.

"Dinner will be ready in five minutes. Just waiting on the

bread," she said, placing the flowers, now in a cut glass clear vase, on the dining room table.

He gave his stomach a rub. "Smells good. Forgive my loud stomach. I've been thinking about this meal since you left and I don't even know what we're eating."

She looked alarmed for a moment, raising a hand to her mouth. "Oh, I didn't think to ask...you don't have any shellfish allergies, do you? I made shrimp and grits."

"Nah, I love shrimp but I've never had it with grits."

"Don't tell me you're one of those weirdos that think grits should have sugar in them?" she said in mock horror.

"Uh, no. Honestly, I can take or leave them."

Noemie put a hand on her chest. "Oh, that's a relief. I thought I was going to have to ask you to leave." She grinned at him. "I hope you like them. I have a secret recipe passed down from my great-grandmother on my dad's side."

A timer dinged.

Rubbing her hands together, Noemie said, "Let me grab the bread and I'll make our plates. Have a seat."

He held up his hands. "I want to wash up first. Where is the bathroom?"

She pointed. "Just down the hall on your right."

Once they were settled at the table with large steaming bowls of food and crusty French bread, they dug in.

Jameson stabbed a shrimp with his fork, his mouth watering in anticipation. Because she was watching he dipped the shrimp in the grits, which he had to admit, looked creamier than he knew grits to be.

He tasted the shrimp, still hot from the stove and grinned at Noemie. Yep, totally worth waiting for. The grits melted in his mouth, the shrimp had a nice kick to it and all of it worked together. He chewed thoughtfully. He could get used to this.

"You made a lot of this, right? Cause I'm going for another round."

"You haven't even finished the first bowl," she protested. "But do you like the grits, or are you just being polite?"

Shoving more shrimp and grits into his mouth, he nodded, not looking up from his bowl. His mother would be appalled at his manners but she wasn't here and the food was excellent.

He came up for air halfway through. "Noemie, this is amazing! I'm serious…I want another bowl." He broke off a piece of the French bread, swirled it around the grits and bit in. *Perfect.*

Realizing she hadn't touched her food, he asked, "What's wrong? Why aren't you eating?"

"I've been tasting it as I go so I'm not as hungry now." She took his bowl and refilled it then nibbled a bit of the bread. "Also, I'm a bit anxious now that you're here, I can't put this off any longer."

Jameson, about to dig in again, stopped eating. "Put what off?" He sat back, wondering what she would ask him to do.

"I'll just spit it out, I guess." Noemie dragged her fork through her bowl, not meeting his eyes.

Finally, she raised her head. "The post office delivered a letter to me today from my dad."

Jameson opened his mouth to ask how that was possible when she continued.

"It was apparently in some dead letter file because the address was illegible but somehow if got forwarded to me from North Carolina." She grabbed her wine glass and took a sip. "Would you review it and let me know what it says?"

"Sure, of course. I know how much you loved your dad. I'll read it."

CHAPTER 11

*N*oemie sighed with relief. Maybe now she could get some food down. There was still lingering anxiety about exactly what her letter from her father might say, but she trusted Jameson to prepare her for the contents.

She took a forkful of the shrimp and grits. Not bad, she decided. Maybe the grits needed a touch more salt.

"I'm kind of leery when women don't eat their own meals. I've seen too many of those forensic shows," Jameson admitted, forking a shrimp. "So, it's good to see you eating."

She tore her focus from critiquing her food, frowning and prepared to defend herself when she saw he was grinning at her. He liked to tease her, she recalled. "Well, I don't know if I can really eat much in this dress. I don't want to burst out of it."

His eyes roamed her body, lingering at the deep valley of cleavage created by the pushup bra the sales rep talked her into buying. Normally the blatant scrutiny from men annoyed her, especially when she was trying to get her point across, but tonight, in this dress, she felt sexy and desirable.

She'd splurged on the dress and the pushup bra and the other items she bought just for him. He was staring at her, the meaning in his eyes clear. He reminded her of a golden tiger in the wild, setting its sights on its unwitting prey then overwhelming it.

"You look good in it. But you must know that." He polished off the last of the shrimp and grits then took a long drink of the wine. "Did you wear it for me?"

Noemie took a sip from her glass. "Maybe."

"So, is this supposed to be our one night?" he asked, pushing his bowl away then resting his arms on the table. "What if one or both of us want more than just one night?" His voice barely above a whisper. He took her hand, rubbed the knuckles. Noemie's knees became weightless from his touch and his words.

As much as it pained her to reveal her truth, she had to be honest. "I don't know if I can give you more than one night."

She wanted to tell him about her ex, tell him her deepest fears but she sat there, silent.

"You can't or you won't?" he asked, releasing her hand. "Is there someone else back in Charlotte?"

She shook her head. "No." There had never truly been anyone else. Only Jameson. "I don't want to lead you on. I just...I don't know."

"What don't you know about, Noemie?"

"Everything. I'm not in a good place to think about a new relationship. I miss my dad...I'm worried about my mom, I... I just don't have the space in my brain right now."

Jameson stared at her then nodded. "Ok. I promised I'd review your letter. I'll do that and go."

Noemie knew she'd hurt him. She saw the moment the wall went up around him. This was all her doing. She might be the reason he never opened up to anyone again.

And now she was asking him for favors. She got up to retrieve the letter from her bedroom with mixed feelings. What if the letter contained bad news or his decision to oust her from the family?

Before his death, she and her father hadn't been on good terms. Ever since she'd broken away from the Jehovah's Witness faith, her father had made it clear she was making the worst decision of her life.

The letter was probably another plea for her to reconsider her break from the faith and to come back.

She found the battered, dirty letter on her nightstand.

Seeing her dad's scrawling handwriting, now smeared and faded, Noemie almost broke down then, but she squared her shoulders and walked back out to the dining table.

Jameson was in the kitchen, rinsing off the dinner dishes when she returned. "Oh, you don't have to do that. Leave them in the sink. I'll load the dishwasher in a minute."

"Least I could do since you cooked." His tone was casual, like he'd talk to a coworker he didn't know well.

Noemie wanted to shake him, beg him to…to what? Have sex with her? Love her like she loved him? How desperate was she right now?

Love her like she loved him.

She wasn't over him.

All this time, she was convinced she had gotten over Jameson, or rather she tried to convince herself that she was over him. Seeing him in the flesh again had awakened all of those old longings and desires for him that she hadn't gotten to experience since she was in college.

Sometimes she wished she cursed. She could curse about her predicament till she was hoarse and maybe she'd feel better.

Noemie sighed, placing the letter on the table and tried to

ignore how good Jameson looked in her kitchen washing her dishes, like they were a married couple.

He looked at her, dried his hands on a dish towel folded on the oven and picked the letter up. "You sure you want to do this right now? I can come by another day."

"That would just torture me. Let's get it over with."

He started to say something, then slid his finger under the envelope flap.

"Let me get more wine first. This calls for wine," she said, grabbing her glass from the table.

She poured the red wine into her glass and motioned to him asking if he wanted more. He shook his head.

"Let's go to the couch. Bring your wine. This might require sitting." Jameson gestured toward the living room.

So bossy, Noemie thought, leading the way to the couch and sitting stiffly on one end.

He sat, and started to read the letter to himself.

There were two pages and once Jameson was finished with the front and back of the first page, he read the second then turned to the back.

Noemie sat with her hands in her lap, scared to interrupt. Jameson's expression remained stoic and she drew the worst conclusion she could. He was disowning her, calling her the worst daughter on the planet.

He smiled at one point.

She was dying to ask why he smiled but she stayed silent so he could read the whole letter.

He turned back to read the first page again.

Finally, after what Noemie felt was a lifetime, he put the pages down and looked at her.

"It's a good letter. Nothing bad. I think you'll be happy at the end. When did your dad pass?"

"Last spring. He had a heart attack." A wave of deep loss

passed through her body and she wanted to curl up on the end of the couch. And maybe she would after Jameson left.

"I'm sorry, Noemie. I really liked your dad, even though he never thought I was good enough for you."

She smiled faintly. Her dad didn't think any of the men she brought home were good enough for his baby girl.

He picked up the pages of the letter. "This is dated March 1."

To my Noemie,
You are my greatest accomplishment. When I look at you, I see the best qualities of your mother and me: you are headstrong, independent, smart, and you go after what you want. You care about people and bend over backwards to help everyone around you without asking. You've always been that way.
I hate when we clash. That same headstrong stubbornness that you got from me has been used against me more times than I like to count. That's ok. I would expect a daughter of mine to challenge her father when he may be wrong.
As I get older, I see the error of my ways.
I know my time is short. Not anything concrete that a doctor has said, just a feeling in my soul that my mission here is coming to a close.
I have made peace with that. I've lived a good life, loved a wonderful woman and had the best daughter a man could ask for. Even though she has chosen her own path, I'm still proud to call you mine.
Seek out your happiness, Noemie. For a while now, I've felt like you have given up on seeking the joy life has in store for you.
You should be loved, cherished, adored, but you have to be open to receiving that love. Don't close yourself off.
Yes, sometimes, opening ourselves up leads to pain, but it also leads to happiness.

I have been with your mother since we were in high school. I knew the first time I laid eyes on her she was the girl for me, and right then I vowed to make her my wife.

Of course, the road hasn't always been easy and as you know, marriage isn't a walk in the park, but it's worth it. I wouldn't trade a day with your mother for all the riches in the world and I want that for you, my daughter.

Just because your first marriage didn't work out doesn't mean you should give up on finding your person.

Keep your heart and mind open and forgive your dear old dad for being stubborn.

Call me when you get this letter. I want to hear your voice and apologize properly.

XOXO,

Your Dad

Noemie sat still, fighting the tears back, her eyes stinging with the effort.

Her dad wanted her to call him so that he could apologize. He was the most stubborn person she'd ever met but he wanted to apologize. And she hadn't gotten the letter. She hadn't called.

She had assumed she had more time and hadn't made any effort to talk to her father.

The tears wouldn't be held back any longer.

She moaned, the sound coming from the pit of her stomach as she let the first drops fall onto her cheeks.

Once the tears started, they kept coming, running down her face, streaking her carefully applied makeup.

She felt Jameson's arms around her and she buried her face in his massive warm chest.

He rubbed her back, told her to let it out, assured her he was there.

Oh Lord, she sighed, she was making a mess of the man's sweater. She was pretty sure this wasn't what he had in mind when he accepted her dinner invitation.

She attempted to pull away, but he held her closer. He felt good, she realized. He smelled like clean laundry and a spicy aftershave and Jameson. She felt protected, cocooned in his arms with him methodically rubbing her back.

The tears slowed as Noemie sighed again.

She really needed a tissue. Or twelve. She must look a hot steamy mess right now.

"Tissue…in the bathroom." she murmured into his damp sweater.

He was slow to release her but he got up and returned with a box of tissues.

Noemie blew her nose, tried to wipe her face. She couldn't imagine what her makeup was doing now. She'd applied more than she normally did, in an effort to look like she didn't have on any.

Now she could probably give a clown a run for his money.

Jameson returned to the couch, concern etched in his features. "Better?"

She nodded, not wanting to speak. A calm settled over her as she replayed her father's final words to her.

Noemie let out a shuddering breath.

He motioned her over, back into his arms. She hesitated for a second, thinking she really shouldn't but then she gave in. He scooped her against him like she weighed nothing before she could open her mouth to protest.

Noemie laid her head against the wall of his chest, let his thudding heartbeat soothe her and let go.

She shouldn't get used to this, her bitter inner voice admonished her. *He'll find a reason to leave again, then where will you be?* She closed her eyes, willing the inner voice to pipe down. He may be gone tomorrow but she wasn't going to fight tonight. She was tired of acting like she was ok and coping with her loss like an adult.

Tonight he was offering comfort and Noemie was being selfish and taking it.

"Hey," he whispered close to her ear. "I'm going to shift my arm a little, ok? You still comfy?"

Noemie nodded then swallowed so she could speak. "Yeah." She cleared her throat. "I should make some tea."

"I'll do it. I saw the kettle on the stove. Where do you keep the tea?" He shifted so that he could lay her against the back of the sofa.

"Cups are in the cabinet to the left of the sink, tea is in the one to the right." Noemie rested her head on the couch, already missing his warmth and the steady rhythm of his heartbeat. "Thank you, Jameson."

She heard the cabinets open and close, heard him run the water into the tea kettle then the tick of the gas stove as he turned on the burner.

He was the first man to grace her kitchen since she'd moved in, she realized.

"Sugar?"

She smiled. "I prefer 'darling' or 'baby' actually."

He stuck his head out. "Ha ha ha...do you want sugar in your tea, Darling?"

The endearment warmed her way more than it should have. "A half a spoon, please."

The kettle sounded and she heard him open and close two drawers before he found the silverware.

He presented her with a teacup and saucer then eased himself back into the couch.

Sipping her tea, Noemie exhaled. "I never called him," she

confessed, her voice raw, "to say I wasn't mad or that we were ok. We never got to have that moment."

"What happened?" Jameson placed a palm on her back, making her lose her train of thought for a moment.

"He was nagging me to go back to Kingdom Hall, you know that's the place of worship for Jehovah's Witnesses. I told him I had no interest in it and he basically condemned me to hell. We yelled at each other, which was unusual for us." She sipped her tea again, reliving that last phone call. "My mother and I were the ones that butted heads and my dad would be the peacemaker."

"That letter was dated March 1, which was the day we argued. I remember thinking he was starting the month off by telling his daughter she was hell bound. In like a lion." She shook her head. *Why hadn't she been the bigger person and called her dad?*

"I guess he wrote that letter later on that day." She sniffled, close to tears again.

The thought of crying made her remember Jameson's damp chest. She sat up, turning to face him fully. "You should probably take off that sweater, but I, oh maybe I do have something you can wear. I have some donations of undershirts for the kids."

He smirked at her. "You trying to get me out of my clothes, Darling?"

She knew he was teasing her with the whole "darling" thing, but it still sent her heart into overdrive when he said it. "I know you can't be comfortable sitting in that sweater."

He shrugged, sat up and pulled the sweater over his head. Underneath, his white tee shirt rose up, revealing a taut brown torso. Noemie forced her eyes back up to his face, which was proving to be harder than looking away from a train wreck.

She licked her lips.

Her intention was simply to tug Jameson's t-shirt down over his stomach but when her fingers inadvertently brushed his skin, she felt a jolt of pure awareness surge through her.

She raised her eyes to look at him. The deep brown eyes staring back at her conveyed his pleasure at her touch. Encouraged, she ran her hand lightly up his stomach, marveling at the ripples of muscles under the thin shirt.

Jameson groaned, covered her hand on his chest with his then brought it up to his lips, He kissed the tips of her fingers, sending little shockwaves of pleasure straight to Noemie's center.

He took a fingertip in his mouth, enveloping it with his lips and Noemie lost the power of speech. She opened her mouth, not sure if she intended to protest or moan or scream.

His lips captured another fingertip and Noemie whimpered. If he could elicit this reaction from merely sucking on her fingers, she couldn't imagine what his lips on her most sensitive parts would do to her.

She decided in that moment she was going to find out.

For once, she would be Noemie the Reckless. Yes, they'd just agreed to take things slow and be friends first, but tonight she was letting her body take charge.

Wait, what about condoms? She didn't have any. Ok, maybe, Noemie the Sensible was a better choice.

Jameson placed a kiss on her palm as she caressed his face with her other hand. She leaned in to kiss him, pressing her lips on his.

Compared to their hasty, heated kiss in the gym, this one was slow, sensual, and thorough.

Noemie savored the taste of him, still familiar after all the years. The faint hint of cigarettes was gone, she assumed he'd quit the habit years ago, but the essence of Jameson remained. Soft, full lips expertly exploring her mouth, teasing her at every turn.

She leaned back, breaking the kiss. "Will you...can you stay tonight?"

Jameson held her face in his hands. "As long as you need me to."

CHAPTER 12

Grabbing her teacup, Jameson pushed himself up from the sofa, intent on refilling Noemie's tea. He tested the kettle water and turned the stove back on to reheat it.

There was still that large beast in the room that needed to be addressed. They weren't seeing eye to eye on how they moved forward.

He was clear. He could see himself proposing to her on her birthday.

Unfortunately, he could also just as easily see her cutting and running for the hills while he was on one knee.

Not ideal.

So, he'd give her time to adjust. Not a lot of time, neither of them was getting any younger, but he could be flexible. He also had to give Jordyn a chance to get used to the idea of a stepmother. That might take time but she had told him he needed to find someone to love.

Noemie appeared in the doorway of the kitchen.

She looked worn out and something else that he couldn't

put a finger on. Not angry. Determined, maybe. Was she spoiling for a fight now because of their kiss?

"You said you liked the dress, right?" She approached him.

"I do. Good color on you." He didn't know where she was going with the question. Better to play it safe.

"I have yet another favor to ask," she said, getting closer. "Would you mind helping me get out of it?"

Now she was just torturing him. "Sure." He'd promised to stay but he wasn't sure how much self-control he'd need tonight. "Turn around?"

Noemie turned, holding her hair up. Jameson unhooked the dress then slid the zipper down to the small of Noemie's back. She should be able to take it from there. If he continued, the dress would be in a pile on the floor and Noemie would be on her back with her legs wrapped around him.

He inhaled sharply at the thought. He didn't need that visual at all. Not helping.

"There. You good?" She was standing too close. He could feel the warmth of her skin close to his. He wanted to touch her again, run his hands over her back, slide the dress off.

The kettle whistled, startling them both.

Jameson flicked the stove knob to the off position and turned to retrieve her cup from the opposite counter but Noemie put a hand over his. "I don't want any more tea right now."

He nodded, unable to take his eyes off her. "Ok, what do you need me to do?"

She reached behind her, slid the rest of the zipper down and shimmied the dress down her legs. She stepped out of it, revealing a matching red pushup bra and panties that left little to the imagination.

Jameson's throat went dry, all of the blood rushing to the center of his body, rendering him hard and ready.

She crooked a finger at him, giving him a look that scorched his skin.

Not sure if he was dreaming, he couldn't move for a second.

Then he couldn't get his hands on her fast enough. Jameson pressed Noemie against the counter then lifted her so she was sitting on it, her thighs on either side of his body. He ran his hands through her hair, tilting her face up to his so he could plunder her mouth.

She opened for him, running her hands down his back, lifting his shirt. He paused the kiss to tug the shirt over his head in one quick motion. Almost skin to skin.

Noemie arched, her breasts pressing against his chest. Jameson wanted to slow down but each touch left him wanting more, faster. He wanted to feel all of her, let his hands and mouth explore every curve, the way he'd fantasized for the last twenty years.

He bent his head to taste that valley her push up bra created that had been taunting and teasing him since she'd opened the door.

Another heave of her breasts against him. Jameson pushed the cups of the bra down, freeing her hardened nipples. He salivated thinking about how sweet they would taste then ran his tongue over one. Noemie gasped then moaned, her hands wrapped around his head.

Jameson wanted the bra out of the way. Hell, all of the clothes the two of them still wore were in his way. He'd take care of the bra first, he decided, reaching behind her to unhook the lacy garment. It was nice to look at, but it had to go.

Once the bra was loose, he watched as she shrugged out of the straps, tossing it toward the dress.

He took a second to gaze at her. "You're beautiful, even better than I imagined."

She ducked her head. "Thank you. So are you."

He lifted her from the counter. He had plans for her that required full range of motion.

"I'm not too heavy?" she asked as he stalked toward her bedroom.

"Nope. You see me struggling?"

"Just making sure." Kissing his neck, she breathed, "I kinda like being carted off like a cavewoman."

Once they reached Noemie's bedroom, Jameson lowered her onto the bed then tugged the red thong down her legs.

The full moon shining through the partially closed blinds provided the only light in the room, but Jameson thought it was perfect. Noemie's brown curvy body appeared to glow in the moonlight. He wanted to touch her, taste her everywhere.

"Even better than I thought," he murmured, placing a trail of kisses starting at the base of her throat. He paused at the swell of a breast, toyed with a nipple until he heard her whimper then continued down to Noemie's stomach.

He stroked her thigh, dragging a lazy finger up to her heat. She parted her thighs, granting him entry and he stroked her with two fingers, loving the way she arched from his touch. There was no way he was going to let her go after their one night.

No way.

He quickly replaced moist fingers with his tongue. He wanted Noemie to know she was cherished. And she was his. Jameson suckled, sucked, teased, tongued, until Noemie stiffened then cried out, speaking the Lord's name in vain as her release came.

She shuttered, her breath coming in quick spurts as Jameson eased back up, needing to be inside her.

Making quick work of removing his pants and boxer briefs, he peered at her as he lowered himself beside her.

He rested his forehead against hers. "You good?"

Noemie nodded slowly, her eyes closed. "Mm-hmm."

She opened her eyes, put a tentative hand on his erection. "Please tell me you have protection?"

"Much to my chagrin," Jameson sighed, "my daughter asked that very question before she let me leave the house. It was like listening to a female version of myself and it was, as she likes to say, epic cringe." He ran a lazy palm up her arm, enjoying the softness of her skin. "But yeah, I do."

"Ok," She slid her hand down the length of him, causing Jameson to exhale like a deflating balloon.

He made quick work of sliding on a condom from the wallet in his discarded pants then he settled between Noemie's thighs, thinking he could stay right in that spot for the rest of his days.

She raised up to put her arms around his neck. "I've waited so long for this…but part of me wants to prolong the moment…I'm sure that makes no sense."

He nodded. "It does." He kissed her nose. "Does it help to tell you I bought a lot of condoms so we can have a lot of moments?"

Noemie chuckled. "Not at all, that's such a man thing to say." She wiggled against him. "Let's get this first *moment* out of the way."

"Whatever the woman wants. I'm just the talent…" He positioned them back against the bed and slowly pressed in to her body, allowing her to adjust to his size.

Noemie's soft sigh in his ear brought chills and Jameson had to force himself to slow things down.

They found their rhythm, Jameson deciding he knew exactly what Noemie meant by wanting to savor the release. He wanted to bring her to the edge over and over again making sure she knew he was staking his claim, establishing that he was the only man she wanted.

Deepening his stroke when she uttered his name, Jameson felt her nails scrape down his back until she reached his ass which she gripped.

For the second time, Noemie stiffened then threw her head back and Jameson felt her release surge through her body moments before his own.

Spent, Jameson flopped onto Noemie's bed, needing a moment before getting up to dispose of the condom. Noemie had her back to him. He placed a kiss on her shoulder then dragged himself up and into the bathroom.

When he returned a few minutes later with a warm, wet face towel, Noemie was huddled under the covers, fast asleep. Oh well, they could always shower together after they got some rest, he shrugged, dropping the towel off in the bathroom. Much better option in his opinion. When he returned to Noemie's bedroom, he kissed her forehead and climbed in beside her.

This, he sighed quietly, he could get used to.

What the hell was that buzzing noise? Jameson raised his head from the pillow, attempting to locate the sound. He looked around, disoriented for a split second, then realized he wasn't in his own bed. The buzzing stopped, allowing him to check on Noemie. Still asleep.

He sat up on his elbow, taking everything in. The sun hadn't made an appearance yet and the room was chilly.

Jameson yawned, intending to burrow back under the down comforter and Noemie's warm body but the buzzing started up again. His phone, he realized, was in his pants that he'd hastily shucked the night before.

Easing out of the bed, careful not to disturb Noemie as she slept, he located the vibrating pants and plucked the phone from the pocket. He checked the number, relieved it wasn't his daughter's and answered, his voice low.

"What's going on, Vanessa?"

"Jordyn's not answering her phone. Can you wake her up for me?"

Huffing in frustration, he checked the time.

"Why? It's not even six...where are you?"

"I'm with my fiancé in Vienna and I want to talk to my child. I'm looking at a bridesmaid dress that would be perfect but I need her size. Would you get her and put her on?"

Jameson ran a hand over his head, willing himself to calm down. He also didn't want to reveal to his ex that he wasn't home. "Vanessa, you realize the time difference? She's still asleep. I'll have her call you when she gets up."

Noemie yawned. "Jameson, everything ok?"

"Who was that?" Vanessa asked, suspicion in her tone.

"I'm at the gym," he lowered his voice, glancing at Noemie. "I will tell Jordyn to call you. Enjoy Vienna." He ended the call then scooped up his clothes scattered across the carpeted floor and hustled into the bathroom for a quick shower.

Noemie was sitting up when he emerged from the bathroom. "So, I guess I'm not the only one trying to keep things under wraps?"

He sighed. "It's not like that. I didn't want to get into where I was with Vanessa. She was already spinning out of control because Jordyn wasn't answering."

"Ok. You sure that's it?" She searched his face. "You seem like you can't wait to get out of here."

He flashed what he hoped was a convincing smile. "Everything's fine. I'm gonna go before she calls back. I know you're on break so you should go back to sleep. Get some rest."

Jameson watched Noemie's face fall. He knew he was earning "that asshole" title right now but he needed to put some distance between them. As much as he wanted to crawl back in bed and assuage her fears, right now he couldn't. "I'll, uh, call you later, ok?"

Noemie nodded slowly. "Sure."

Then she turned onto her side, away from him. "Can you lock the door on your way out?"

Shit. "Hey, Noemie, don't do this. Don't push me away." He wanted to touch her but he wouldn't risk her rejection.

She huffed, flipping over to face him and Jameson knew she was about to let him have it. "I'm not the one pushing people away. You said you needed to go, so go talk to your ex-wife. I'll get some rest, as you suggested."

Jameson ran a hand over his face. "I didn't mean it like that. I've gotta go change and open the gym." He sighed. "It would be nice if I could concentrate on that and not on you being mad at me."

Noemie sat up, covering herself with the comforter.

"I want to say I overreacted, but it's deeper than that." She wouldn't meet his eyes. "I don't think I can do this again, Jameson."

His heart thudded in his chest. He rubbed his beard. "So, we're done before we even give it a chance? Is that what you're saying?"

"Better to know this now rather than later, I think." Her voice was soft yet firm.

"Why?" he said, crossing his arms, challenging her logic. "You give me one good reason why."

He cocked his head to the side, waiting. "Last night was how I want us to be...eating together, supporting each other, sharing a bed, all of that."

"Until we don't. And you decide that you don't want me anymore, like you did twenty years ago. You led me on that summer. I had to find out from your pregnant girlfriend that everything you said was a lie."

Jameson unfolded his arms, dropping them at his sides. "None of it was a lie. I loved you then, I just didn't know how to tell you about her. I thought we were done until she told me she was pregnant."

Noemie turned away. "I guess you want a medal for not leaving her and your child." The bitterness in her voice was like a fist to Jameson's gut.

"No, I don't want a medal. There was no way I wasn't going to be present in my child's life." Jameson sighed, realizing he was fighting a losing battle, "Noemie, this is our chance. I'm not saying we can pick up where we left off that summer, but I'm here, you're back home, you can't deny you have feelings for me. I never stopped loving you."

She looked at him with unshed tears in her eyes. "It's not enough, Jameson. I don't know if I can trust you with my heart again."

"So that's it? You don't want to give us a chance?" His voice sounded raw to his own ears. "Noemie..."

He walked over, attempted to touch her and she flinched like he might strike her.

"I can't," she said softly. "I just can't."

CHAPTER 13

*C*lick. Noemie tried unsuccessfully to still her pounding heart as she listened for her front door to close. He was gone.

She could stay in bed and cry now.

No, she couldn't. First of all, she was still naked. She never slept naked and now that Jameson was gone, she imagined this was how Eve felt after biting that apple. Exposed.

Noemie sighed and dragged herself from her warm empty bed. The man had only been in it a few hours and already she missed him in her space. The sheets smelled like him, which made her want him back near her ever more.

Why did she think she could walk away from Jameson after their one night? Was she really that naïve? Wincing as she padded into the bathroom, she knew a long hot bath was in order to ease her soreness and hopefully, clear her mind.

Adding her favorite bath salts to the oversized tub and checking the temperature as the water flowed into it, Noemie's mind drifted back in time, replaying their night. She'd gone from crying tears of grief and guilt to tears of joy in the span of a few hours, thanks to Jameson. Before last night, she hadn't thought it was possible for her to orgasm, let alone multiple times.

Now she knew.

She wanted to know if her lack of sexual desire was her or her partners and last night had proved it wasn't her at all. It was as if all the pressure they'd built up trying not to give in to their longings had built up until it finally flowed like a burst dam. She and Jameson hadn't been able to keep their hands off each other, experiencing multiple *moments* until they were too tired to move.

Noemie sank into the scented water, letting the bubbles cover her. Why wasn't she ok this morning? She should be riding the high of good sex and multiple orgasms, not sitting in a tub alone on the brink of tears.

Why had she been spoiling for a fight first thing? If their roles were reversed and her ex was calling, she would walk over molten lava before she admitted to him that she was in another man's bed. He had no right to know.

Could she really blame Jameson for not telling his ex-wife the truth? She didn't know the whole story.

Or was she being naïve and getting in too deep, setting herself up for more heartbreak?

"I never stopped loving you."

His words rang through her head.

She ran her hands through the bubbles in the tub, created a landscape of mountain valleys and peaks, The act was soothing and allowed her mind to drift, drilling down to the most basic thing she needed to know.

Had last night been a mistake?

Noemie pulled up in front of her childhood home and sighed. The house looked the same as it always looked, but there was a shabbiness about it now that she hadn't noticed before. It seemed like it was succumbing to its age. Her mother lived in the small ranch all by herself now. She was always asking Noemie when her current lease was up so that she could move back home. Noemie had no plans to do that. She liked having her own space. Plus, her mother wasn't the most agreeable person and her irritability seemed to get a little worse each time Noemie stopped by.

As her mother aged, Noemie knew there would have to be a decision made about her care but she'd cross that bridge when she came to it.

She was in rare form that day. Her mother, typically posted on the couch where she had the best view of the street, met Noemie at the front door. "You need a better coat, Noemie! You're going to catch pneumonia. Come in here and stop letting the heat out."

"Hey Mama, nice to see you, too." Noemie gave her mother a half hug and started into the living room.

Her mother grunted. "Nothing nice about the day. It's too cold for my old bones." She hobbled back toward the couch after opening the door for Noemie.

Now that she was there, Noemie wondered not for the first time why she'd decided to visit her mother that day. She wasn't in the right frame of mind for her mother's pessimistic views but she wanted to ask about the letter from her father. Telling her mother about her situation wouldn't help; the older woman never liked Jameson.

She sighed. She was here now, might as well make herself useful. "Mama, you want coffee? Or tea? I brought some shrimp and grits I made; want me to heat it up?"

"Your grits are usually too lumpy for my taste, I'm fine.

You don't need to hover, sit down." She peered at Noemie over her glasses. "Are you heading back to Charlotte to spend Christmas and your birthday with your friends?"

Noemie did as she was told, taking a seat on the couch, her hands in her lap like she was being scolded. "No, I'm staying here."

"I assume you're observing both?" Her mother peered at her.

Noemie considered the question. While she no longer considered herself a religious person, she liked the traditions that went along with the Christmas holiday. She'd decorated a tree and made her apartment look more festive but she hadn't made plans for the holidays or her birthday.

"I'm acknowledging my birthday and Christmas but I don't have any plans, if that's what you're asking."

Her mother leaned back, lacing her fingers. "I wish you'd consider coming back to the Hall, but that's all I'll say about it."

She twisted a bangle bracelet on her left wrist. "Mama, did Dad tell you he was writing me a letter after we had that big argument?"

Her mother took her glasses off and used the hem of her shirt to clean them. "A letter? No. Your father wasn't a letter writer."

"Yeah, he wrote me a letter that same day but I guess they couldn't read the address. I just got it a couple days ago."

The older woman shook her head. "He didn't say anything about it to me. Probably because I would have told him he was wasting his time. You kids don't read letters. Too busy on those phones."

She peered through the glasses then shrugged and slipped them back on her face. "What did it say?"

"He apologized," her voice cracked. "He told me to call

him so he could say it in person. But I never did."

She clucked. "Noemie, your daddy was the most stubborn person I ever met. He made my blood boil most days with his 'my way or the highway' attitude, but I loved him anyway. And he loved you. You were everything to him. He knew your heart just like you know his. Don't let one little argument trouble you."

Noemie nodded. "I miss him, don't you?"

Her mother chuckled. "He hasn't left! His spirit is still around here driving me crazy." She sat back, resting her arms on her stomach. "Before you send me to the old folks home thinking I'm losing my mind...I dream about your father most nights. In my dreams we have long talks, most times about you, and I wake up feeling like he's right there beside me again."

"What do you all say about me?" Maybe she should get her mother's mental state checked more often. And why hadn't her father appeared in any of her dreams?

"He thinks you need to find a good man and get married again. He told me I should help you find one but I told him I was too old for that nonsense. I suggested maybe you could get on the computer and find one, you know that's how Mrs. Schmidt found her husband, but he's old; I don't think you want a man that old, anyway, your dad didn't like that idea."

Noemie sat with her mouth slightly agape. What was her life right now? "You all are discussing my love life in your dreams?"

She guessed that answered her question about why she hadn't dreamt about her father; he was busy trying to control her love life from beyond the grave.

"Wasn't my idea." Shrugging as if it was no big deal, her mother reached for the television remote. "You know how bossy your dad was. He hasn't changed."

CHAPTER 14

*T*oday is the first day of the rest of my life. Noemie
rolled her eyes. She had always hated that saying.
She knew, technically, it was true but she didn't need to be
reminded of it.

"Happy Birthday to me," she said, looking at her reflection in the mirror. Her skin was still smooth, although she
did notice a small frown line between her eyebrows. Maybe
she should smile more. She chuckled. Nah. She couldn't go
from what Teresa had called her 'resting witch face' to
smiling all the time. People wouldn't know how to react.

What was the plan for today? She glanced around her
apartment. There were things she could be cleaning or organizing but she didn't feel like doing that.

She stood in the middle of her apartment, reflecting.
Somewhere along the way, she'd stopped striving for excitement and adventure and this week of new experiences she'd
planned was showing her just how boring her life was.

What happened?

She had given up, that's what happened. Noemie had let

her broken heart convince her that she didn't need to feel or get out of her comfort zone.

Since it was her birthday, she was going to do all of the things she wanted to do that day and a hot coffee with all the trimmings she usually denied herself was first on the list.

Walking back to her bedroom to throw on clothes for her coffee run, she sniffed. Jameson's scent, clean and male, lingered. Noemie closed her eyes, recalling her words when he left.

There was a part of her, the hopeless romantic part, that thought maybe Jameson would come back at some point with a gift for her, ignoring her declaration that they weren't going to work. That small part wanted him to fight for her, for them, but he'd left that morning as soon as she'd declared she couldn't trust him with her heart.

Could she?

It wasn't like she'd ever stopped loving him.

He was more mature now, not as impulsive. He went after what he wanted.

That was the thing.

Jameson always pursued his goals with relentless drive but he wasn't pursuing her that way. Did she want him to?

Maybe. She frowned.

Yes, her heart insisted.

He should have fought for her.

She sat on her bed and thought about the statement.

That's what was stopping her. He hadn't shown her that he really wanted to be with her. He'd said as much, but her father had always drilled into her that it wasn't the words you believed, it was the actions.

She slid on a pair of worn, comfy jeans and a sweatshirt with a new determination. Noemie wasn't going to sit and brood all day; she was going to take action. Well, as much action as one could take the day before Christmas.

She was pushing her feet into her sneakers when a knock at the door interrupted her.

Noemie's heart raced, hoping it was Jameson again.

She checked the peephole.

A delivery woman held a large bouquet of red and white flowers accented with silver ribbon and sprigs of holly berries. Noemie unlocked the door and greeted the woman.

"Saint, right?" The woman checked her phone, not looking up.

"Yes, that's me."

The woman nodded, passing Noemie the phone so she could sign with her finger.

She tipped the woman and wished her happy holidays as she held the bouquet. A white card stuck in the middle caught her eye and she pulled it out of the envelope to read it.

"Happy Birthday to the woman who stole my heart twenty years ago - JM"

Noemie pressed the small envelope to her chest.

Her finger grazed a hard object in the envelope. Turning the envelope upside down, Noemie shook it, causing a small key to tumble out.

She picked up the key. It looked like it would fit a music box.

While she fussed with the flowers, fluffing out the petals, and enjoying the delicate feel of them between her fingers, she heard another knock on the door.

Reluctantly she rose, placing the key on the table near the flowers.

The same woman appeared at the door, this time with a brown box that looked like it might hold a pair of shoes. Had he bought her shoes? The idea, while a bit odd, was intriguing. Noemie tipped the woman and took the box to the table. Using a knife to break the packaging tape, she opened the flaps and removed a silver antique keepsake box.

The box had her initials, NLS, on it.

Noemie sighed. When they had gone on their first date, Jameson had a million questions. No one had ever been so focused on her. Maybe she missed the attention, she thought wryly.

"Noemie Crawford, huh? What's your middle name," he'd asked, giving her this look that she couldn't read. She had hesitated, wondering if she should be giving a strange boy, no matter how cute she found him, her full name. Weren't there identity thieves ready to steal her information?

"I'm not trying to stalk your or anything, I'm just curious," he'd raised a shoulder like he was a little embarrassed. "I want to get to know you."

"Liliane. My mother was taking French when she had me," Noemie explained. "They went to Paris a few years ago."

"Maybe I'll take you to Paris one day, if you're lucky." He winked at her, sending heat running up her neck over her cheeks.

"You'll be the lucky one, if I decide to go. I actually speak French." She realized a beat too late that he was flirting with her when she looked up and caught the look in his eyes. That look made her want to clutch her proverbial pearls, and at the same time, lean into him.

She did neither, choosing instead to cup her hands in her lap.

Noemie blinked the memory away. So he remembered her middle name. Not that big a deal.

She placed the key in the lock on the memory box and turned it. Inside was a smaller box and her throat caught for a moment until she realized the box was too large to be an engagement ring.

She pushed the tiny seed of disappointment aside, not wanting to deal with it. Of course, she wasn't ready to be engaged. They weren't really even speaking right now.

The box contained a silver bracelet, identical to the one her father had given her as a high school graduation present. "Silver represents purity, strength, clarity, and focus." Her father clasped the thin chain on her small wrist, his face solemn, as if he were trying to hold back tears. "All things you need to be the independent woman we've raised you to be."

She nodded, running her fingers over the precious metal. "Thank you, Daddy."

She'd lost the bracelet shortly after she'd married. Her husband didn't like her wearing jewelry that he hadn't purchased so she kept it in a jewelry box on her nightstand. They had a break in one weekend while she was out of town visiting her parents and the thief had stolen the jewelry box.

Noemie always thought the burglary was too convenient for her taste, but she never raised the issue.

Now she picked up the bracelet from Jameson, holding it up so that it sparkled in the sunlight streaming in. The piece was beautiful, thicker than the original but very similar.

Noemie put the bracelet on and willed herself not to cry. *How did he even know?* She got up to make herself a cup of coffee when the doorbell rang again. This time she wasn't surprised to see the same delivery woman.

"This is the last one. Happy holidays," the woman said as she handed Noemie a large padded envelope.

Again, Noemie tipped her and thanked her.

She ripped open the package.

Inside were a pair of women's flannel pajamas adorned

with dancing reindeer. She pulled a sticky note out and read it.

Wear me immediately

She unfolded the set, grinning. They were corny, but the size looked right. Looks like her coffee run would have to wait. Noemie stripped out of the jeans and sweatshirt and slipped the new set on.

Back in her bedroom, she admired the set in the full-length mirror. Not a typical birthday gift, but she liked them. The reindeer were cute.

There was a knock at the door and Noemie's heart thudded. The delivery woman normally rang the bell. The knock sounded familiar. She ran back into the living room, checked the peephole, then flung the door open.

"I see you got my gifts. Happy Birthday." Jameson stood there, a lopsided Santa hat on his head, grinning at her.

Noemie just stared, her heart pounding. *How could she deny she wanted this? Him?*

"Um, can I come in and put this stuff down?"

Snapping out of her thoughts, she realized he was carrying a duffel bag and what looked like food in paper bags. "Thank you! Oh, yes, sorry," she stood aside so he could enter.

As he strode past her, she also noticed he was wearing a pair of dancing reindeer pajamas just like hers under his jacket. She couldn't contain her excitement. "What is all of this?"

He hefted the bags onto her dining room table then plopped the Santa hat on her head. "Well, this is what I call Christmas in a Day."

Once his hands were free, he took hers. "I see you followed directions. I did a great job with the size. Anyway, I know things didn't go well that last time I was here but I wanted to do something special for your birthday. We're packing all of the normal Christmas activities into one day," he released her hands and took off his jacket, "starting with pajama selfies."

Noemie laughed. "Oooo, I get to take pictures with my silver Santa, but I'll need coffee first. And makeup."

He took out his phone and set a timer. "You look good without it. You've got five minutes before the camera goes off; we've got a busy day planned."

Noemie turned on the coffee maker then sprinted to her bathroom where she rubbed on a tinted moisturizer, her favorite lip stain, and swept a coat of mascara on her lashes. Then she took off the Santa hat and her head scarf, gathering her hair in a low side braid. She placed the hat back on.

Jameson called out, "Your five minutes is up, do I need to come in there?"

"Nope! I'm ready," she announced, moving toward the kitchen to prepare her coffee.

Once she had the cup in hand, he held up the phone and posed them beside her Christmas tree, with his arm around her shoulder. Noemie hoped she looked as happy in the pictures as she felt. Her heart rejoiced in his presence.

After a few more pictures, he got to work warming up their Christmas breakfast and shooed her from her own kitchen. "I can help, you know."

He planted a kiss on her forehead. "Nope. It's your day. Go sit. You're going to need your energy today."

She started to insist on helping then thought better of it. He was right.

Jameson called her to the table and set a hot plate of pancakes, scrambled eggs and bacon in front of her. She rubbed her hands together. "This looks amazing!"

Noemie located a mini bottle of maple syrup in one of the

bags, swirled it on her pancakes, and then sliced a piece. The fluffy pancake melted in her mouth. "Where did you get the food from? This is probably the best pancake I've ever had."

"I made everything this morning. Glad you're enjoying your food."

She nibbled a piece of crispy bacon. "So, what are we doing after breakfast?"

"Heading to Louisville," he said, placing a champagne flute with orange juice next to the plate, then watching her. "You're like a kid on Christmas morning."

"Well, yeah. I was going to get a holiday coffee concoction for breakfast and call it a day. This is a million times better."

He topped the glass off with champagne while she watched, impressed. She hoped he hadn't planned for them to go out that evening. She wanted to stay in and show him her appreciation properly, which might take all night.

Jameson sat down across from her, preparing to eat.

Their eyes met. He put his fork down. "Noemie, eat your breakfast and stop looking at me like that."

She blinked, all innocence and naïveté. "Like what?"

"Like you want to rip my clothes off and press me against the nearest wall," he said wryly.

Hmm. Not a bad idea. Sipping her mimosa, she decided to be bold. "Is that an option?"

His deep brown eyes flashed. "Normally yes, but not right now. We have a schedule to keep. So, eat up and get dressed."

"Yes sir," Noemie mock saluted.

Once Noemie finished her food and showered, she emerged to see Jameson dressed in a heather grey sweater and dark jeans. She considered suggesting he leave the pajamas at her house but that was presumptive of her.

The drive to Louisville would take about an hour and on the way, Noemie tried to guess what they would do for the rest of the day. Jameson told her they had a packed schedule which had her curiosity fully piqued. She felt like a kid on their way to Disney for the first time. "So, you won't give me a hint?"

"I gave you a hint back at your apartment. I told you to dress warmly," Jameson said, taking his eyes off the road to glance her way.

"That doesn't narrow it down. It's cold out. A better hint would have been 'bring a swimsuit'."

"Well, there's another hint. You don't need a swimsuit today."

She rolled her eyes. "How long will we be in Louisville?"

"Long enough. Not overnight."

Not helpful at all.

Eventually, he pulled into the parking lot of the ice arena.

"Ice skating?" She gawked at the building. "I don't know how to ice skate, do you?" she asked, turning to him, trying not to panic.

"Yep. I played hockey for a season." Jameson grinned at her. "You're in good hands."

And somehow, Noemie knew she was.

True to his word, Jameson was patient with her, staying close in case she fell, or so he said. She suspected it was so that he could touch her as much as he wanted. Not that she was complaining. She was having a wonderful time.

They skated until Noemie said she'd had enough. Jameson then took her to a fancy hotel that offered afternoon tea and a hot chocolate bar. The hotel's lobby area had a grand fireplace with a crackling fire to set the mood and several plush comfy chairs for guests to feel the warmth.

Even though the hotel was busy and several families had turned out to take advantage of the gourmet hot chocolate, Noemie and Jameson were able to snag a velvet bench to the right of the fireplace. Noemie sat with both hands cradling her mug of raspberry hot chocolate.

Jameson laid a hand on her leg. "You having a good time?"

She beamed at him. "Eh, it's aight."

He pursed his lips.

"I'm kidding...this has been the best birthday ever." She took another satisfying sip of her hot chocolate. "What are we doing next?"

CHAPTER 15

*J*ameson grinned at Noemie, unable to keep the relief that she was having a good time out of his voice. "We're heading back to Kissing Springs but we have some down time before our next activity. Anything you need to do today?"

Noemie thought for a moment. "Not really. But can we stop at my apartment for a minute? I want to change."

He nodded. "Sure, we can head there now."

Noemie asked a server for a to go cup for her hot chocolate while he downed his. He waited for her in the lobby and when she strode to his side, on impulse, Jameson took her free hand in his.

He could celebrate her birthday with her like this for the rest of his life.

But he got the distinct sense she wasn't ready for a conversation like that.

"I know you didn't celebrate holidays as a kid, but what about when you were an adult? Didn't you celebrate with your husband?"

She sipped her drink. "I told him early on that I wasn't used to celebrating my birthday and he took that as he didn't need to make a big deal about it. So, he'd get me a gift and tell me Happy Birthday but we focused on Christmas Eve more. We always went to his family's gatherings where we'd spend most of the day there waiting on the food to be prepared."

She winced. "I dreaded going. His mother didn't think my cooking was up to par. That was the first thing I celebrated when the divorce was done. No more dry Christmas Eve gatherings."

"So, what did you do for the holidays after you called it quits?"

"Nothing much. Sometimes I'd hang out with friends and sometimes I just spent it at home by myself, which probably sounds lonely to you, but I see it as freedom. I am not obligated to attend someone else's gatherings. If I want to, I can, but I can also enjoy my own company."

His heart warmed that she'd chosen to spend her special day with him. "Well, I'm glad you decided to play along today. How's the big 4-0 feel so far?"

Noemi fingered the silver bracelet. "No different than thirty-nine. I am realizing that I need to embrace life more. This was perfect, Jameson, thank you."

"Oh, don't thank me yet...day's not over," he said, rubbing his hands together.

"That sounds oddly ominous?" She tilted her head at him.

He laughed. "I didn't mean it to. I don't know why I'm so excited to go do basic things. We're going to see the Lights Over Kentucky show tonight, then dinner at Two-Four-teen...that's the grand plan."

"Oh, I've always wanted to do that but I was never here for the holidays."

They piled into Jameson's truck and headed back to Kissing Springs.

Noemie was quiet and Jameson wondered what she was thinking. He glanced at her out the corner of his eye. "You ok over there?"

"Yeah, I'm...fine. Your questions about my marriage had me thinking."

"Oh, I didn't mean to put a damper on the day, I was just curious. You should have told me to mind my business."

She waved a hand. "No, no, you're fine. I just realized how unhappy I truly was and how I wasn't appreciated even though I was doing all the things I thought a good wife and daughter-in-law was supposed to do."

Jameson wanted to pummel her ex and his family at that point. She took care of everyone else and no one was taking care of her.

"I don't know if your mother ever said anything to you but after my divorce was final, we only lasted three years, I heard you'd graduated. I asked your mother how to get in touch with you and she told me you'd just gotten married."

The woman seemed to take pleasure in delivering the devastating news to him but he saw no reason to tell Noemie that.

Noemie turned to him, frowning. "She never mentioned it." Her head swung back to the window. "That explains some things she said to me over the years though."

"Were you at least happy initially?" he asked softly.

The only sound in the car was the engine and the holiday music station.

Noemie didn't face him. "No. I was in love with someone I couldn't have."

He huffed in frustration. All the years wasted with both of them in miserable marriages.

"Noemie, is it too late for us?"

She turned then to look at him and he blurted, "Actually, don't answer yet. Really think about it and let me know later."

When they arrived back at Noemie's apartment, Jameson checked the time. "It's a little after four. We have dinner reservations at seven then the light show at nine. We have a little down time."

"I think we have just enough time for a classic Christmas movie." She picked up a remote control and spoke into it. "Alexa, play Die Hard."

The television blinked on and the movie started.

Jameson rolled his eyes. "Ok, I love Die Hard as much as the next man, but I'm sorry, it's not a Christmas movie."

"I mean, it takes place at a company Christmas party, what more evidence do you need?" She set the remote down on the coffee table. "Do you want anything to drink? Popcorn?"

"I'm supposed to be serving you today. Do you want another mimosa? There's champagne left."

"That champagne is probably flat by now. But no, I'm good." She sat on the couch tucking her legs under her.

Jameson put an arm around her shoulders pulling her in close, enjoying the coconut scent of her hair.

The last thought he had before he drifted off to sleep was that he could see himself growing old with this woman in this same spot.

"Hey, Jameson, wake up!" Jameson felt Noemie nudging him but he didn't want to open his eyes just yet. He was dreaming of Noemie on top of him, the Eiffel Tower visible from their bed, his hands stroking her bare breasts as he thrust his hips, deepening the stroke.

"Are you awake? We're going to be late for our dinner reservation." She was sitting up on the couch, pointing at a clock on the wall above the television.

Jameson groaned, tried to get his body under control. He was painfully hard and regretting their birthday plans. Dinner had seemed like a perfect idea at the time but right now all he wanted to do was carry Noemie to her bedroom and recreate his dream scene, minus the Paris setting.

"One of us needs to jump in the shower first," she raised her eyebrows at him. "Do you want to go?"

"Only if you come with me."

Noemie side eyed him hard. "I don't think we'll make it to dinner if we do that."

He glanced up at the clock. "it's just now six. I'll call Tucker and tell him we're going to be a few minutes late and you," he rubbed the back of her neck, pulling her toward him for a kiss, "get in the shower. Get everything warm and wet for me."

Her eyes darkened as she caught the meaning of his words.

As soon as Noemie left the room, Jameson pulled out his phone and called his friend Tucker Jackson, head chef and owner of Two-Fourteen. "Hey, Tucker, we're running a little late tonight, can you still seat us if we get there around eight?"

Tucker snorted. "Yeah, whenever you two come up for air, your table will be waiting."

Jameson knew his friend was going to continue to give him a hard time about the delayed reservation but he didn't care. He ended the call and placed the phone on the table, eager to join Noemie in the shower.

He stripped like his clothes were on fire, piling everything onto a chair in Noemie's bedroom, and stalked toward the sound of running water. Anticipation had him practically salivating at touching and tasting her skin.

Noemie was wrapping her hair up, keeping it in place with the bobby pins she held between her lips. Her arms were raised as her hands molded her hair, causing the short satin robe to ride up and gape open. He didn't think it was possible for his erection to get any stronger, but the view of her smooth brown thighs and barely concealed hard nipples almost sent him over the edge.

He tugged at the robe, pulling it off her shoulders. She dropped her hands and the robe slid soundlessly to the floor.

They might not make it to dinner.

Noemie wrapped a satin scarf around her head, tying it tightly then slid a shower cap on. He watched her with a smirk. The pink shower cap was adorable on her.

She pointed at her head. "My only request is that you don't get my hair wet...unless you plan to flat iron it before we go to dinner."

His eyes slowly perused her body, plotting out where his hands would explore first. "You're standing in front of me naked and beautiful taking all my breath away...you could ask me for anything right now and it's yours."

Biting her lip, she tilted her head at him. "You certainly know how to charm the panties off a woman."

"I'm only interested in charming yours off," he said, sliding the glass shower door open. Steam escaped, enveloping Noemie like she was ascending from the heavens. "Shall we?"

She stepped into the shower first and Jameson followed her in, pulling her into his chest and running his hands over her breasts, down her stomach, stopping to part her lips and tease her clit. She exhaled sharply.

Jameson nibbled her neck then whispered, "Not my normal MO, but we need to make this quick. Pass me your body wash."

She plucked the bottle from the shower caddy that hung on the shower head and handed it to him, then Noemie turned so that she and Jameson were chest to chest. She took him in her hand and stroked him, then after a moment's hesitation, dropped to her knees and took him in her mouth.

Jesus, Mary, Larry and Temika, he was going to explode. The combination of her hot mouth on him and the warm water running over their bodies had him wanting to do a praise dance. He started to push the shower cap off her head but remembered her one request and touched her shoulders instead.

"Come here," he growled, tossing the body wash down and taking Noemie's face in both hands. His lips possessed hers, claiming her, expressing how much he cherished her.

Jameson needed to be inside her right then. He ran his hands down her slick, wet body and grasped her ass, lifting her from the ground and pivoting them so that her back was against the wall. He held her firm with one arm while he guided his penis toward her. Noemie arched, spreading wider for him as she held on to his neck. He thrust into her warm wetness and she cried out.

They moved fast and hard like they were battling to see who could make the other come first. Jameson felt Noemie's body tighten around him and he lost it as she jerked, calling his name. He buried his face in her neck as his orgasm ripped through him.

He wanted to slide down the shower tile to the floor but they had reservations. The shower was now only lukewarm as Jameson bent to retrieve the soap. He squeezed some into his hand and ran it over Noemie's skin, enjoying the slick flesh. Their eyes met before Noemie's fluttered shut as he slid his palms over her breasts. She arched her back and he cursed his meticulous planning. Jameson wanted nothing more than to make love to her again

She grabbed the soap from him and did the same starting with his massive chest.

Once they were as clean as they could be given the cool water and frequent distractions, Jameson reluctantly stepped out of the shower first and plucked a fluffy towel from Noemie's linen closet to wrap her in. They shared another searing kiss as they toweled each other off.

He was finding it impossible to keep his hands off her, Jameson thought, rubbing the towel over her legs. He'd have to focus if they were going to make it to dinner and the surprise he'd planned with Tucker.

She disappeared into her closet and Jameson flopped on her bed once his clothes were on so that he could put on his shoes. The gravity of his situation hit him like a tire iron to the skull. He didn't think it was possible but he was more in love with Noemie than when they were in college. The depths of his feelings now scared him. He'd been able to walk away then. There was no way he could do that now.

Noemie strode out of the bathroom, fastening a dangly silver earring to her ear. Jameson noticed she was wearing the bracelet he'd picked out for her. "You ready? We should go."

CHAPTER 16

*W*hat a difference a week made, Noemie marveled as she pretended to study the menu. Everything looked good and she'd heard from the teachers that the food was excellent. She kept sneaking looks at Jameson, who seemed to be oblivious to her stare.

They were sitting in a round booth toward the back of the restaurant in a section catered to diners that craved privacy. The lighting was low and a candle flickered on the center of the table. Super romantic setting made for lovers.

A week ago, Noemie was convinced that sex was over-rated, at least to her, and she thought she'd be content if she didn't have it for the remainder of her days. Now she was contemplating a quickie in the ladies room.

Funny how quickly Reckless Noemie had taken over.

Jameson leaned in, nuzzling her jawline. "I got caught up in the moment back in your shower. We didn't use anything…"

"I'm on birth control."

He nodded and she was probably imagining things but she got the sense he was disappointed.

Noemie put the menu down. Her goal had been to have her one night with Jameson which had turned into twice that. She wanted him to stay tonight but didn't know how to broach the subject.

He also said he had another surprise for her and the curiosity was killing her. What if he pulled out a ring and popped the question? That couldn't be it, but what would she say if it was?

A week ago, she was certain her answer would have been a polite but firm "no."

But now, her answer wavered between "Let me think about it" and a "yes, let's throw caution to the wind."

Seriously, Reckless Noemie?

But if she thought about it, it wasn't the worst idea in the world. Or the afterglow of amazing sex and the best birthday ever had her questioning her stance on marriage.

She fingered the silver bracelet he gave her. The man had good taste, he was kind and cared about the town. He'd make some woman happy. That thought gave her pause, had her catch herself before she went down a dark path imagining Jameson making love to another woman in the shower.

Maybe that woman should be me.

"You can't be that engrossed in the menu," Jameson said, resting his arms on the table.

"I'm not, just thinking about things."

He went still. "Anything I need to worry about?"

"No, what makes you ask that?"

"Just making sure you're ok. You got quiet on me which means you're thinking hard about something."

She studied him, realizing he was just as vulnerable as she in this moment.

He cleared his throat. "I'm gonna just put this out there. This isn't a casual thing for me. I've waited twenty years for you without consciously knowing that I was. I dated a bit but never got serious with anyone, mainly because I made raising my daughter my top priority. Now I realize I was comparing those women to you all along."

His words warmed her and terrified her at the same time. "What happens when the real, flawed me doesn't live up to the version of me you've had in your head all these years?"

Jameson shrugged a shoulder. "You pretty much shattered that image that day at the school. I was irritated that you waltzed back to town judging the best thing to happen to this town in years but I found the attraction was still there." He stroked his chin. "And I was maybe checking out your assets a little too hard."

She was the last person to judge; she had thoroughly ogled him that day.

"We're all flawed. I happen to love the real you, flaws and all."

She was afraid to trust his words. She wasn't that young, naïve girl he'd known that would take people at their word, trusting them only to have them betray her. She had thick, fortress like, ivy covered walls up and she guarded them ruthlessly.

But at some point, maybe when he'd let her cry into his chest, or when they'd taken selfies in their Christmas pajamas, or when he spun her around the ice rink holding her tight so she wouldn't fall, she'd let one of the walls be breached.

How are you so sure?

She hadn't realized she'd said the words out loud.

"I've seen you ready to spit fire at me, I've held you while you mourned your father, I've been inside you and felt when you came. I'm not saying I know your every mood, but I want to. I want us."

Maybe she did too.

Before she could agree to "us" she needed to come clean. "Jameson, I need to tell you something."

He gripped her hand. "Ok." His eyes searched her face. "This sounds serious."

"I married a very religious man after college. I committed to my faith and tried to bury myself in it. I went to Kingdom Hall several times a week and I volunteered and taught the members. I did all of the things. Then when I got home, I tried to be a perfect wife so I was cooking and cleaning, all of it."

Noemie wanted to weep for her younger self, trying to please everyone to the detriment of her own happiness.

"I knew my husband expected me to fulfill his physical needs but I never questioned what my needs were and if he was fulfilling them. Spoiler alert: he was not. But I didn't know anything about my body or how to tell him what I wanted. So, I didn't and for the longest time, I just thought I was the problem. I didn't care that much for sex."

The words she spoke about her feelings seemed so foreign to her now.

"The women at school told me I was uptight and needed to have more orgasms."

Jameson's eyebrows shot up but he said nothing.

"So, when you saw me holding that...toy, I was thinking about buying one, not that one," she amended quickly. "So that I could see what I was missing. Then when you offered to help, that seemed like a better way to figure out if it was even possible for me to have one."

"Wait a minute, that night at your place when you seduced me, that was your first orgasm...ever?"

"Yes, it was." She realized what he'd just said. "And I certainly didn't seduce you."

"You sure? You were all big brown eyes saying, 'help me out of this dress' and "stay with me tonight' knowing I couldn't resist you." He used a high-pitched voice as hers.

"I'm pretty sure I didn't sound like that."

"I have to work on my Noemie voice more. So have you changed your mind about sex now?"

She rested an arm on the table then put her chin on her fist, her eyes conveying her meaning. "Ever since we sat down, I've been thinking we could sneak off to the ladies room, lock ourselves in a stall and get a quickie in before dessert."

His eyes darkened as they watched hers causing her nipples to react as if he'd run his thumbs over them. "I'm thinking about it. Tucker's never going to let it go though." He took her hand. "But as soon as we're alone, you're all mine."

All mine.

The words sent the most delicious chills through her.

Jameson had arranged a three-course tasting menu for them. The food was excellent and Noemie was ready to curl up on the couch with Jameson and ring in Christmas day.

Later, after the multi course dinner and birthday dessert of the best chocolate cake Noemie had ever tasted, she felt like she might burst.

She had to be the luckiest woman in this world right now, she thought as she leaned into Jameson's side. The night had gotten cold and blustery but there was no snow predicted.

Jameson put an arm around her as they waited for the valet to retrieve his truck. "You ok? Still having a good birthday?"

"Yep. Just a little too full and cold." She rubbed her hands together to warm them.

"Well, I told you I'd handle the rest of your cake if you needed me to."

"You would have polished it all off if I'd let you. It's supposed to be my birthday," she said, shaking her head.

"It is your day. I was helping you eat it so you wouldn't feel like you needed to finish it."

She glared at him as he lifted a broad shoulder. "I'm helpful, what can I say?"

He pulled a bag from behind his back. "And I snagged an extra piece for later."

Her eyes went wide. "I guess I can keep you around, assuming we're sharing that piece."

He lowered his voice. "We'll share it after I get you home and get these clothes off you."

Noemie almost licked her lips in anticipation.

She watched as the young man pulled Jameson's truck up to the curb where they were huddled together.

The valet jumped out to open her door. "Happy birthday! How was your meal with us this evening?"

Taken aback, Noemie smiled at the man. "Thank you! It was wonderful." She reached into her purse to tip him, even though she knew Jameson had probably already done so.

Noemie clicked the seat heater on and settled back to enjoy the ride. She wanted more nights with Jameson, talking together, laughing, teasing and loving each other.

"So," he said, reading her mind, "did you still want this to be a one and done deal?"

Before she could answer, his phone rang, the tone reverberating through the car's speakers. "Hey Ma, what's up?"

"Son, I need to tell you something but I need you to

promise you won't freak out." Carla's voice held none of the joy it normally had when Noemie talked to her.

"Freak out about what? Did something happen?"

"Promise me you'll stay calm, Jameson?"

"Ma, the more you say that...you know what, fine, I'm calm."

Noemie rubbed his arm, letting him know she was there for him.

Carla let out a quick sigh. "Jordyn had too much to drink and Izzy's mom took her to urgent care to make sure she didn't have alcohol poisoning. You need to go pick her up from Izzy's. You can bring her here."

Jameson gripped the steering wheel. "She what? How much did she have to drink? She's only nineteen!"

"Son, you have to calm down before you get to Izzy's. Jordyn didn't want anyone to call you because she knew you'd react like this, but Izzy's mom felt we needed to know."

Noemie's heart went out to him. She rubbed his arm. "Do you want me to drive? Maybe pull over for a minute..."

He cut her off. "No, no, I'm fine," his tone was brusque. "Ma, Izzy's on Adams Street, right? White house on the corner?"

"Yes, that's right. Jordyn's car is there. Is that Noemie?"

"Yes, Carla, I'm here."

Jameson's voice got louder. "Was she driving? She better not have been behind the wheel."

Carla cut him off. "Noemie, don't let him storm in there like he's lost his mind. Jordyn feels bad enough as it is. You all bring her here and I'll take care of her."

"No, she's coming home. I need to get to the bottom of this. She knows better-"

"Jameson!" Carla whipped the word out, cutting him off.

When they reached the house, Jameson pulled up to the

curb behind a red Honda. "Ok, ok, I'm calm," he said, gritting his teeth. "We're here. I'll call you back, Ma."

He ended the call and cut the ignition. His head hit the steering wheel. "I'm gonna make sure she's ok then I'm going to strangle her."

Noemie ran a comforting hand over his neck and shoulders. "Why don't you wait until morning to grill her about her actions tonight. Just be her dad and take her home."

"Alcoholism runs in our family and she knows this…she's not even old enough to drink. Why would she risk everything like this? No, we're hashing this out tonight."

"Jameson, that's not the way to approach this situation. Maybe you should take her to Carla's for the night then you can talk to her tomorrow."

He turned to her then, his eyes ablaze. "You don't have kids. You have no idea what the right approach is. I'm sorry, you just don't."

Stung by his words, Noemie pulled away as if she'd been burned. "I might not have children but I've been working with kids close to her age for several years now, so I'm well-versed on how they think. And, I was a Daddy's girl, so there's that. But you do you. Go in there and demand answers, make her feel worse than she already does, cause that's always the best parenting move."

Jameson rubbed his forehead. "I shouldn't have said that but I can't deal with this right now. I need to get my daughter."

With that, he got out of the car, closing the door forcefully.

Noemie started to go with him but decided staying in the car was best. Jameson had made it clear he didn't need or want her help. She sat back, her arms folded. He could have left the keys so the car would stay warm, she fumed silently.

Immediately, Noemie's anger cooled. No, she couldn't truly understand how a parent felt in this situation but she could empathize with him. He was likely scared, concerned about his only child, and probably feeling guilt that he wasn't there when Jordyn needed him. Jameson was used to navigating the parental waters alone and didn't need an outsider second guessing his decisions.

Which would always be the case. If they were to move forward in a relationship, she would always be the new person in the equation. Eventually, maybe she would be the stepmother.

Stepmother.

The title made her cringe, thinking of all the bad portrayals of stepmoms in the media. While she didn't think she'd be considered an evil stepmother, Noemie wasn't one who thought parents should be their children's friends. She tended to be strict with her students.

Maybe she wasn't ready for that role.

She turned toward the house when she saw the front door open out of the corner of her eye. A petite, brown skinned young woman, her shoulders bent and arms crossed, walked tentatively toward the truck. Jameson appeared, nodding at a woman, Jordyn's friend's mother, Noemie guessed.

Jordyn stopped abruptly when she approached the passenger side door, her eyes wide. She hesitated for a second then reached for the back door.

In person, Noemie thought as she watched the young woman climb into the back seat, Jordyn looked more like Jameson. At that moment, Noemie realized just how much she envied Jameson's ex-wife. Jordyn should have been her daughter with Jameson.

She turned in her seat to face her. "Hello, Jordyn, I'm Noemie."

Deep brown eyes the same shade as Jameson's studied her.

"You're Noemie?" she finally asked. "My mom said you're the reason they split up. She said he will never love us like he loves you."

Noemie frowned, unsure how to respond. Apparently, she wasn't the only one coveting what the other woman had.

"Were you the side chick or was my mom?" she continued. "Or did both of you think you were the one?"

Noemie turned back to face the front of the car. "As you are probably aware, each person's version of a situation is what they believe to be true but not necessarily the truth. Your father can give you the most accurate version."

"I asked him when I was younger and he only said I didn't need to worry about you, that you were gone," Jordyn said. "He seemed sad when he said it, I think I assumed you had died."

Noemie said nothing, her attention on Jameson as he waved at Izzy's mom and strode back to the truck. He was still scowling when he folded himself in but his voice had none of the hard edge left. "Jordyn, I need to take Noemie home. Do you want to go to your grandmother's house for the night or do you want to go home?"

"Gramma's house," she said in a shaky voice. "Daddy, I'm sorry."

Noemie barely heard the soft-spoken apology but she felt the young woman's anguish. Those three words conveyed how much Jordyn needed her father's approval and acceptance. She glanced at Jameson, her breath held.

"I know, Baby Girl. We'll talk about it after Christmas."

They sat in the parking lot in front of Noemie's apartment, the truck idling to keep them warm. Jordyn was with Jameson's parents and Noemie stifled a yawn, realizing it was nearly midnight.

Jameson, she could tell by the methodical way he stroked his chin, had a lot on his mind. "I shouldn't have snapped at you earlier and implied you don't know anything about raising kids," he turned to her, "hell, you're probably more qualified than I am. I'm trying to figure this parenting thing out day by day."

He took her hand. "I'm so used to doing this all by myself...Vanessa only shows up occasionally to be the fun, cool mom then she's gone...it would be nice to bounce ideas off someone else."

Noemie caught the implications of his words. "You're still sure about us?"

How could he be so sure when she was wound up tight with anxiety, regret, longing, and a million other emotions she couldn't, or wouldn't identify?

Jameson nodded. "I am. But I need you to be sure as well. I realize you never answered my question earlier and maybe it is too late for us, but I'm pleading my case. I fell for you hard that summer and I know it's been twenty years, but my feelings haven't changed. Being with you this week just confirmed it." He removed her glove, stroked her palm. "Yes, I realize we've both changed, but I'm willing to take our time and really get to know each other."

He ran a hand up her arm. "I'm going to go; I know you need time to process things." He slid his coat on, making his way toward the door. "If you're up to it, we all have Christmas dinner around 2:00 at my mom's."

Noemie nodded.

He placed a firm kiss on her forehead. "I love you with all my heart, Noemie."

His words made her heart sing before it sank.

She watched him walk out the door, leaving their future in her hands. Noemie opened her mouth to tell him, tell him what, to wait? That she needed time, that she had never stopped loving him even when she hated herself for doing so?

Fear of letting the last wall she'd erected around her heart fall kept her silent and rooted in place.

She didn't stop him.

CHAPTER 17

*J*ameson woke on Christmas morning to a quiet house. Too quiet, he thought with a jolt, but he settled back into bed when he recalled the previous night.

Jordyn was with his parents.

This, he realized suddenly, was the first Christmas he'd ever spent alone. When he found out he was going to be a father, he was still in college, living with his parents, and he'd gone from being responsible only for himself to being the head of a household with a wife and a new human depending on him.

Jameson stretched. For once, he didn't have to rush to get up and have presents and breakfast waiting. As was their tradition, Jordyn and Jameson would open their gifts and Jameson would make his famous blueberry pancakes. Then later in the afternoon, they would go to his mother's house for dinner and more gifts from the larger family. Occasionally, Jordyn's mother would call her from whatever exotic destination she found herself in for the holidays.

Technically Jameson could sleep in. He rolled over in the empty king-sized bed, wondering if Noemie was thinking about him this morning. She'd never been in this bed, they'd always been at her house in her queen bed but that didn't stop his body from longing for her beside him, cocooned in the comforter.

He missed her already.

Would she choose him and show up for Christmas dinner later on? His gut clenched thinking about the previous night. Something had happened to make her unsure. She hadn't had to say anything, he just felt her retreat back behind the walls he thought he'd knocked down.

As much as he wanted to, Jameson resisted the urge to call her. He'd give her space. He had to trust that she'd see he was ready to be hers.

She wasn't ready.

The mantra kept running through his mind.

He was stubborn, refusing to give in to those thoughts. He looked over at the phone resting on his nightstand. Nope, he wasn't going to call her.

He picked up the phone, staring at it for a few minutes. Then he initiated a call.

"Hey Ma, Merry Christmas. Jordyn up yet?"

She chuckled. "You kidding? I don't expect she'll get up till we're ready to eat dinner. Merry Christmas to you."

His mother paused. "So, Jordyn met Noemie last night. How did that go?"

"I don't know. Jordyn was in the car with her while I was talking to Izzy's mom. When I got in, there was definitely tension in the air. Noemie didn't say why."

"Hmm, you invited her to dinner, right?"

"Yep."

"You think she's coming?"

"No idea."

They spent a few minutes talking, then Jameson told her he'd be by later on and ended the call.

He stared at the phone for a few minutes longer before he scrolled to Noemie's number. He longed to call her but opted to send her a text instead.

Merry Christmas!

I miss you. He started to type the words then deleted them, deciding to keep his texts casual.

He saw the dots indicating she was typing and held his breath.

The dots stopped.

Disappointed, Jameson put the phone down and got out of bed. He wasn't going to sit by the phone waiting.

He would rather pace. As he stalked around the den, picking up things Jordyn had left scattered like breadcrumbs, showing where she hung out, the house seemed to close in on him and he knew he needed to get out. The gym was closed for the holiday which meant he could go work out undisturbed for as long as he wanted.

After layering up in a hoodie, t-shirt and shorts with sweatpants, Jameson headed toward the gym. His gym. The fitness center was a source of pride for him. He'd always had some entrepreneurial venture going on, even as a young boy. He played sports and as a reward for helping his grandmother stock up at the bulk warehouse store, she'd buy him a couple boxes of candy bars and he in turn would sell candy to the other kids in his class from his locker.

He was a natural sales person, always had been. He pulled up in front of the gym and scanned the sign. J&J Fitness. Named for his daughter just in case she wanted to take over the family empire one day.

Thinking about his daughter made him frown again. Was

this overindulgence a regular thing? Was this normally how she spent her time, drinking and passing out?

Now that she was in college in Lexington, he didn't know what she was doing, who she hung out with first hand. He only had what she'd deemed worthy to tell him. He'd talk to her about the drinking.

He realized as he unlocked the door, his breath coming out in small clouds in the cold, that he was thinking about everything except Noemie. But what was there to think about? He had bared his feelings, put his heart out into the universe for her and she'd rejected it. Rejected him.

Do you still want us?

She'd answered his question loud and clear.

No.

And there was nothing he could do about that. He'd thought he could wear her down like he did anyone else who told him no.

His father, Jameson Mitchell Sr, had always taught him that one of the keys to success is to persevere after everyone else gives up. "Son, people will tell you no more than yes in life. They'll give you a million reasons why your ideas won't work. That just means you have to adjust your ideas and keep asking. Each no gets you closer to yes. Remember that."

Jameson left the lights off. He didn't want anyone who happened to be out this morning stopping by thinking the gym was open. And, if he was honest with himself, he preferred to leave the shadows from the morning light in place. It matched his mood.

In his office, he stripped off the hoodie, then set out to warm up with a jump rope. As he jumped, his mind cleared, transporting him back to the first time he'd seen Noemie.

Jameson was sitting in the class, willing it to be over so he could rush over to the basketball court with his friends. He was thinking of his favorite NBA player, Tim Duncan. Not only was Tim one of the best players in the league, he'd stuck it out and finished his undergrad degree, despite intense pressure to quit early for the draft. If Tim Duncan could get his degree, so could Jameson, he reasoned, but he'd need to pass this dry class first

Then she walked in, head held high, and took a seat in the front row, directly in front of the instructor's desk. She didn't look around at the other students, no one acknowledged her presence, but Jameson couldn't keep his eyes off her.

With her dark, smooth skin and slim shape, she reminded him of the African American girl in that chick flick Vanessa had dragged him to, 10 Things I Hate About You, which, he had to admit, wasn't half bad. She turned, flicking a curtain of raven hair over one shoulder, to glance around the room and caught his eye. Her expressive eyes widened and she quickly turned back to face front.

Jameson stroked his chin. Yep, she was stunning and not as haughty as she let on. Not that he was worried. He was tall, athletic and charming as hell. It was just a matter of time before he'd have her smiling at him.

He winced at the sheer cockiness of his younger self as he jumped. He'd thought he had life all figured out back then.

Until that summer changed everything.

Finishing his warm up with a set of jumping jacks and some full body stretches, Jameson reflected on that summer. He met and fell in love with Noemie then found out he was going to be a father within a month.

He'd had to grow up fast after becoming a husband, and a father, then soon after—a single dad.

Jordyn would always be his baby girl but now that she

was becoming an independent woman, it was time for Jameson to find his happiness.

He thought he had.

Jameson heart pumped with adrenaline from the workout but there was also fear driving him. Donning a pair of boxing gloves, he stalked over to the speed bag and started a rhythmic pounding. Sweat beads ran down his face, blurring his vision, but he kept punching, determined to keep his distress at bay.

He'd survive, he assured himself. He'd survived losing her once, he could do it again. And maybe this was for the best. He had a gym to run and expand. He could open another branch closer to Jordyn's school and maybe she'd want to run it with him.

If not, it would keep him busy. Too busy to wonder what she was doing, who she was with while he pieced together the heart she'd rejected.

Jameson gave the bag a final swing then leaned against the wall, spent. He slid down to the floor, his back against the wall, his breath coming in deep bursts.

Sitting on the floor, Jameson rested his arms on his legs and let his head drop between his knees.

Maybe he wasn't ok.

His phone pinged, startling him.

Merry Xmas...open the door pls

CHAPTER 18

*N*oemie stood at the door, shifting her weight from foot to foot, mainly to stay warm, but she also wasn't sure Jameson was at the fitness center, even though his truck, the only vehicle in the lot when she pulled up, was there and still warm.

There were no lights on in the building and the place felt deserted. Or maybe he was in there and didn't want to see her. That realization made her pause. Noemie stood still for a moment, debating. Maybe she was too late and he didn't want anything to do with her. She should go, she decided, stepping away from the door.

The door opened and Noemie turned back to see Jameson stick his head out.

Her heart raced. He was dripping with sweat, but he was there and holding the door open for her. She hurried, not wanting him to be exposed to the cold any longer than necessary.

Nerves battled with the joy of seeing him. She wanted to

run into his arms. They weren't exactly welcoming arms. He had them crossed against his chest at that moment.

She walked past him into the building.

Jameson closed the door and she heard the click of the lock as he secured it.

Now that she was here, she seemed to be at a loss for words. Noemie fidgeted with the knit scarf around her neck.

"I realized I don't know where you live," she said suddenly, "so I came here on a whim, hoping to run into you."

He shrugged, his expression unreadable. "I'm pretty much always here. Not on Christmas normally since we're closed."

"Yeah, I figured the gym would be closed today."

Jameson nodded. They regarded each other.

Finally, Jameson spoke. "Noemie, what do you want?"

His tone was flat. Like he just wanted to get on with his workout. And he wanted to get on with his life. Was she too late?

Noemie heard her father's voice, repeating an expression she heard all throughout her childhood.

Noemie, say what you mean and mean what you say!

"You. Us." She had one more request, a huge one, but she'd let the dust settle on this one first.

"I've gotten way out of my comfort zone this week, probably done more living this week than I have in twenty years. I lived through the sheer embarrassment of you catching me in the adult section with that thing in my hand." Noemie felt her cheeks warm, reliving that scene. "I survived that and then mustered up the courage to ask you for one night."

Jameson raised an eyebrow at her. "Go big or go home, right?"

147

"No, I didn't understand what I was seeing so I pulled it down for a closer look, but that's not the point."

He moved closer, but he didn't uncross his arms. "Ok, what exactly is your point?"

His tone, she noted, had softened. Progress. "You asked if I still wanted us, wondered if it was too late for us. And for years after I found out you were going to be a father, I thought it was." Her shoulder slumped. "I think that was when I gave up on my happiness."

She looked Jameson in the eyes, saw the tension, fear, and love in them. "This week I realized that there's so much I want to do…my father would want me to live the best life I can live, not sit around mourning him. I miss him, I imagine I always will but I needed to push through the rut I was in."

Noemie moved a step closer to Jameson, wanting to touch him. "I hope it's not too late. I'll admit, it's cold and scary outside my familiar bubble of comfort, but I love you, never really stopped loving you and," she sighed, "I'm all in if you still want us."

Jameson let out a shaky breath. "Noemie, you know I'm in. I want to grab you and hug you but I'm sweaty, I don't want to…"

Before he could finish the words, Noemie pulled him, sweaty clothes and all, toward her and kissed him like she hadn't seen him in years.

Jameson pulled away, stroking her cheek with his thumb, his gaze heated. "I'm glad you moved back home. I'm also glad you came looking for me. As much as I hated to, I was going to give you some space to figure things out, but we can take things slow, whatever you need. I'm not going anywhere."

His words filled her heart. "I have another thing to discuss with you," she figured she should just say it.

"If you tell me you ate that whole piece of cake, we're going to have a problem, Ms. Saint."

She put a finger on his lips. "I'm serious." Noemie bit her lip then blurted. "I know your daughter is pretty much grown but how do you feel about having another one? I want to try and have a baby."

Jameson's eyes met hers as he took her hand and kissed it. "Well, I think you should marry me so we can get started on that project right away."

EPILOGUE

One Year Later

Jameson stood still, trying not to move as his younger sister Gia adjusted his bow tie.

"Who knew you cleaned up so nicely? I'm glad you decided to go with this tux." She patted the tie and turned him toward the full-length mirror in the suite. "I like the satin lapels."

He stroked his beard. He did look good. "Of course, I clean up nicely. You know me. You don't look so bad yourself, little sis."

Gia, wearing a dark red chiffon maxi dress, spun on her heels. "Thank you." She posed then tilted her head at him. "You sure you ready for all this?"

He wanted to say he'd waited over twenty years for this moment. "Yep." He leaned in to adjust his jacket. "You know I would have done this last year but Noemie wanted a winter wedding."

"So, her birthday, Christmas Eve, and your wedding anniversary all on the same day? That's a lot of gifts to get."

"Yeah, it is, but you know what, she spent so many years not celebrating any of that, I'm happy to celebrate all of it with her."

Gia punched his arm. "You're so sprung. But seriously, I'm happy for you, Jay."

Jameson retaliated by pinching her cheek like he did when they were kids. "You'll be the same way when you finally settle down."

She swatted his hand away. "No sir. I have a lingerie empire to build. No time for that foolishness."

"Well, I'm glad you decided to open up shop here in Kissing Springs. With all the weddings and bachelorette parties we do here, you'll be opening up new locations before you know it."

"I hope so. I've put all of my savings plus an investment from Mama and Dad into this store. It's got to succeed." She looked at the time on her phone. "Ok, it's almost show time. You ready to meet your bride?"

Jameson tugged on the lapels of his jacket. He was ready. He couldn't wait to take Noemie's hand and recite the vows he'd written just for her.

Later, he stood beneath an archway filled with greenery wrapped with white tulle, staring at a spectacular view of the Ohio River from the top level of the Muhammad Ali Center and waiting for his wife-to-be.

Jameson marveled at the difference a year made. This time last year, he was trying to convince Noemie to take a chance on them, hoping she felt the same way he did. Now, here they were, a year to the day, pledging forever.

He felt jitters rise in his gut. Did he have his vows? What if he messed up the words? Worse, what if he started tearing up like he did when his baby girl graduated from high school?

Shaking those negative thoughts away, he turned toward their friends and family as they filed into the neat rows of chairs adorned with Christmas themed ribbon and greenery. Seemed like everyone in Kissing Springs was here to witness their union.

The wedding party, however, was small; Jameson's father would serve as best man and Jordyn would be Noemie's maid of honor.

His father and best man, almost as tall as Jameson ambled down the aisle and took his place next to Jameson. "I think they are about ready to start. You ready, son?"

"Yeah, Dad, I'm ready."

His father clapped him on the back in approval. "She's a good woman. Just remember, 'happy wife, happy life' and you'll be ok."

Jameson chuckled softly, looking over at his mother who blew him a kiss and waved like he was headed out to sea. His parents' antics calmed him. Even if he tripped over his vows today, he was marrying his forever woman, the woman who was meant to be his wife.

The wedding planner signaled for the guests to rise. The hushed conversations stopped as "I Found You", a song that Jameson loved, started.

Everyone stood. Phones in camera and video mode were held up to catch the bride.

Jameson held his breath as Noemie, flanked by her mother on one side and Jordyn on the other, floated down the aisle toward him.

She looked ethereal in an ivory lace gown, her hair pinned up in looping curls accented with a spray of white flowers on one side. He knew he was the luckiest man on the planet right then.

Jameson watched Noemie pass her bouquet of white and

red amaryllis to Jordyn and give her swollen belly a gentle rub. He grinned. That was his son, reminding them that he wanted to be part of the festivities with enthusiastic kicks.

Noemie beamed at him, mouthed "Hey" as she stood opposite him and his heart jumped. He knew that smile was just for him and he looked forward to seeing it for the rest of their days.

"Your child is acting like my uterus is a soccer field," she murmured under her breath.

"You might as well get used to saying my son because I know it's a boy."

Noemie mock rolled her eyes in response. This was a constant battle between them but Jameson knew she was having a boy even though they wouldn't get to know for sure until the gender reveal shower in a couple of months.

The officiant cleared his throat, eyeing them sternly.

They straightened up and managed to make it through their vows and the rest of the ceremony without incident.

When the time came to kiss his new wife, Jameson tilted Noemie's face up, putting his lips a whisper from hers. "Thank you for choosing us. I love you, Noemie Liliane Mitchell."

WELCOME TO KISSING SPRINGS

Welcome to Kissing Springs, Kentucky!

In this new collection of steamy romance, nine authors bring you standalone stories from single dads to second chances, ex-military to sports romances all set in the small town of Kissing Springs, Kentucky.

You just read Silver Santa, by Joi Jackson.

Read next: Salty Santa, by Annie Rae.

View all the books in the series here.

WELCOME TO KISSING SPRINGS

MULTI-AUTHOR STEAMY ROMANCE SERIES

Welcome to Kissing Springs, Kentucky!

In this new collection of steamy romance, nine authors bring you standalone stories from single dads to second chances, ex-military to sports romances all set in the small town of Kissing Springs, Kentucky.

Coming Soon:

Welcome to Kissing Springs: Sunshine Season, Summer 2023

Welcome to Kissing Springs: Bourbon Season, Fall 2023

THE WELCOME TO KISSING SPRINGS SERIES

ACKNOWLEDGMENTS

I loved writing this book. Noemie and Jameson were such fun to write and I'm excited to write Jameson's little sister Gia's story next.

First, I have to thank my husband Steve for indulging me when I would randomly throw a scene idea or character trait at him and expect him to respond immediately. He knows me pretty well after twelve years of marriage but maybe he can't read my mind. We'll have to work on that.

To my partner in crime and Clubhouse hostess extraordinaire Satia Cecil, I couldn't have gotten this far without your help. I've learned so much from you over the years and I continue to be in awe of your creativity. I appreciate you and look forward to our next big thing together.

To the other Welcome to Kissing Springs authors, Grace, Kristin, MR, Britney, Tracy, Anne, Ellen, thank you all for your help and guidance and feedback! Looking forward to our Summer and Bourbon series!

To Zee, thanks for bringing this idea to fruition! You inspire us all and I can't wait to see your writing career explode beyond your wildest dreams.

ALSO BY JOI JACKSON

The Love, Lies, and Catfish Series

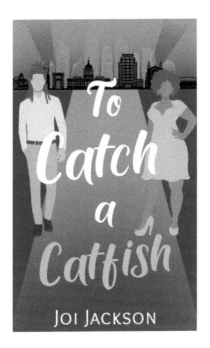

Book 1 To Catch A Catfish

Book 2 Catfish in Paradise Coming in 2023

Lightning Source UK Ltd.
Milton Keynes UK
UKHW011010070223
416609UK00006B/1630

9 781736 316399